To A

CW00767774

Pomp
and
Circumstances

✝

Sue Hampton

[signature]

PNEUMA SPRINGS PUBLISHING UK

First Published in 2012 by:
Pneuma Springs Publishing

Pomp and Circumstances
Copyright © 2012 Sue Hampton

Sue Hampton has asserted her right under the Copyright, Designs
and Patents Act, 1988, to be identified as Author of this Work

Pneuma Springs

British Library Cataloguing in Publication Data

Hampton, Sue.
  Pomp and circumstances.
  1. London (England)--Fiction. 2. Young adult fiction.
  I. Title
  823.9'2-dc23

ISBN-13: 9781782281818

Pneuma Springs Publishing
A Subsidiary of Pneuma Springs Ltd.
7 Groveherst Road, Dartford Kent, DA1 5JD.
E: admin@pneumasprings.co.uk
W: www.pneumasprings.co.uk

Pomp

and

Circumstances

To my dear husband

ONE

James woke without the usual help. No shouts from downstairs, no knock on the door and no complaints or threats. He breathed out hard, as if the night had been an effort. But in fact he'd crashed out and slept through in one long stretch. *Effort* didn't cover an evening with Eleanor Langridge, one-to-one. It was his first date, and he'd needed to blank it. As far as Eleanor was concerned, it was definitely the last.

At eight twenty-nine, outside the restaurant, came the first missed kiss. Standing aside for Eleanor to walk in ahead, James noticed her hesitation. With a clientele as young as the waiters and music to fit, he'd thought the place was safe. The last tomato-stained high chair was being wiped and folded up as families made way for groups of student-age friends, and couples who seemed casual, established, easy. But from the start, his evening was full of empty pauses, pricked now and then by jagged conversation.

"I don't normally go to pizza places," she said, to the cutlery.

James let his eyebrows do the talking. It was a trick that amused his sister Faith, but Eleanor didn't seem to notice. Mainly because she was preoccupied with the fork, angling it like a diamond – found in a cesspit.

"It's dirty," she said.

"I'll have it," said James, and reached for it. She gave it up with a puzzled, *oh, pur-lease* sort of look without a trace of gratitude. As if the bacteria had transferred themselves across the table to James himself.

"My English grandparents had a dog that ate mess from the ground," he said. "It didn't come to any harm – well, until it died."

She frowned.

"Is that a joke?"

"The dog isn't laughing."

James felt bad then, because he'd been fond of Benji. But Eleanor didn't spare any sympathy. She was putting on her glasses and inspecting the menu as if it was covered in stains and someone should take samples to a lab. Eleanor wanted to do sciences for A Level, and be a pathologist.

James remembered Olly saying Eleanor should be on a Spec Savers ad, looking clever and classy.

"I'll have a salad," she said. "No dressing."

The up and down look she gave him suggested that he might have taken dressing a bit more seriously himself. Eleanor couldn't have looked much more stylish if she was meeting an aristocrat for cocktails at the Savoy. In fact...

"My dad says you should be on standby tomorrow," he told her, but as she lifted her head and removed her glasses he knew it was a mistake.

She squinted briefly. Now James felt like a stain himself.

"Sorry?" she asked.

James lost confidence in everything – including the other kind of date. Was it tomorrow? What was the bride's name?

"At the Royal Wedding?" he tried. "In case she doesn't turn up..." He looked down at the menu himself, even though he always chose the same: dough balls with mozzarella, followed by a marguerita and the cheesecake to finish. "He meant it as a compliment."

Eleanor fixed him hard. He felt like a cucumber slice being speared.

"I'm not twenty-nine," she pointed out. "And my mother wasn't an air hostess."

James noticed that she didn't deny her father's million (or two).

She hardly agreed with anything all evening. And James was used to that, with Faith, but Faith grinned while she retorted or contradicted, and cushions got thrown and dodged. The insults muttered or lobbed were crazily inventive. It was different with Eleanor, who didn't seem amused, or even measurably annoyed. She spent more time looking at her shoes than her date.

Eleanor had the strange good looks of another life form with super-human style. But James decided she was flatter than the pizza he planned to enjoy – while her glare tried to make it decompose. He nearly asked her whether she had a little sterile bag on her, and offered her a corner to take away for analysis. Would his saliva be a bonus?

Eight thirty-nine. That was when James gave up on any kiss at all.

His alarm clock showed that it was almost exactly twelve hours later. The light through his curtains was pale and when he pulled them apart there was no sign of the sun. His dad, a running, cycling weather watcher, would call the outlook "iffy."

James heard the TV launched downstairs. Just because it was an oversized flat screen, his sister seemed to think the volume should fill a cinema. But there was no dance beat, so someone else was watching. This was confusing, because his mother, Agnetha, should be at work. And even though his father had been made redundant a few months ago, he always took himself off to his study at seven each morning to scour the Internet for jobs.

James felt sticky. Sniffing his armpits, he found Eleanor had made him sweat. Stepping into his en-suite bathroom he remembered that most of the holes in his shower head were blocked by limescale and no one would bother to do anything about it until his mother left a note for Kim Chung when she came to clean on Tuesday.

As he crossed the landing, Faith jumped out of her bedroom. Eyes and mouth widening, she hurled herself into the bathroom before him, slammed the door and locked it behind her. Faith was always complaining that she had no shower of her own, but until their father found another job, there wasn't much chance of their four bathrooms becoming five.

James looked through the open door of his parents' bedroom. He didn't like using their en-suite, which was the biggest, newest and flashiest, because he felt like a tabloid journalist.

His friend Olly called his mum a Swedish blonde – which was accurate but supposed to mean a lot more. Things were different for Olly, who had a step-mum and a step-dad now. Sometimes James felt vulnerable, having still-married parents – as if most of the other volcanoes had already erupted and he could be a resident of Pompeii with no inkling of what was to come.

He squeezed too hard with Agnetha's shampoo and there was no end to the whipped cream lather. James almost broke bones sliding around in it as grunts and groans escaped through steam. On his dazed head foamy peaks rebuilt themselves every time he tried to knock them down. It was no way to start the day. Exhausted, he left the shower basin looking as if his mother had been whisking up a soufflé in it.

Rubbing the clouded mirror with the base of a fist he saw the redness of his flesh and eyes. James tried to remember why he'd got up at all. What day was it? His Easter holidays had run for ages but he hadn't done as much revision as he'd intended. Maybe he'd draw up a timetable. The new term started next week, after the May Bank Holiday. His father, Stephen, said the money they paid for his independent school was an investment.

Even before his dad joined the jobless, James didn't like the pressure that word implied. Expectations of him. Assumptions that he'd make the investment pay off. He hadn't sat his first exam yet and already his father was pushing for *"ideas"* about the future. James didn't have any, and preferred to take each day as it came: a single unit – and usually challenging enough.

James supposed the foam would disappear one way or another and Eleanor might know the scientific verb for the process. He realised he was thinking more about Eleanor now than he ever had before he'd asked her out. It hadn't been planned, exactly, before her mother started giving him lifts home just because they lived five minutes' walk away. "You like everything easy and convenient," his father told him recently. "Yeh?" was one response, lifted in a way that meant, *Of course. Doesn't everyone?* His father didn't lose his temper. He just let his slow in-breaths get the message across. Concern. Anxiety. Disappointment at the ready.

James didn't expect to do brilliantly in his GCSEs but he supposed he'd do all right. "Why isn't all right all right?" he asked his mother once, because she was very precise about her English. "Doesn't it – y'know, by definition – have to be?"

Emerging from his parents' bedroom in his dark blue towelling robe, he could still hear the TV downstairs. He banged on the bathroom door.

"What's going on?"

Faith opened the door, towel-drying hair that was shorter than his. "Out the way!" she cried, her English being less precise and way more American. "It's starting soon."

"What is?"

Faith pulled a face that meant he was ridiculous. "Do you *know* what day it is?"

James thought maybe Saturday but reconsidered. "Friday," he said.

"Any particular one? As in global event and national holiday?"

Their father was on the stairs, in his cycling gear. It was hard to tell whether he was on the way out or back from a ride because he never looked damp or hot and his chest didn't sag or puff.

"Your brother's life's one long holiday," he commented, and seemed to be heading for the shower James had just left behind. James tried a tactical disappearance.

Passing the lounge, he saw crowds on a street being interviewed by the BBC Breakfast sports guy, and his mother eating a bowl of muesli in front of the screen.

"Ah," he said.

"Big splash as James falls in," said Faith, dressed for summer. She joined their mother on the sofa, two blonde heads focused together. "He had no idea what day it was."

Royal Wedding Day. Eleanor hadn't seemed excited at the prospect. He couldn't imagine her breakfasting in front of the coverage. She'd have done hours of revision by now.

Faith's ring tone sounded. She sprang up and slipped down to the other end of the lounge, facing the back garden.

"People are going crazy," Agnetha told him. "They're lining the streets already."

Faith seemed to be going slightly crazy too as she listened to one of her friends. Even looking at her back, James could see the animation mounting until her bare feet left the ground and she let out a squeal.

"Cool!" she cried, like fizz released from a can. "Yeah! Later!"

"Hyper," muttered James as his sister almost long-jumped back to the sofa.

"We're going to Buckingham Palace," Faith announced. "Meeting in ten minutes at the tube station so there's no time for an inquisition."

Nice try, thought James, and couldn't be bothered to listen in to the exchange that would follow: Agnetha being firm, reasonable and caring, and Faith trying cute and appealing until it failed and she ran upstairs to slam her bedroom door. His sister was only thirteen but her life seemed to be an ongoing battle to win total freedom, and every time she lost one round she seemed even more determined to win the next.

Pouring himself some cereal in the kitchen, James looked up to see Faith blowing him a kiss. But it didn't occur to him that it meant goodbye until he heard the front door close a couple of minutes later, about the same time that his mother called, "Keep in touch!"

"You let her go!" he rebuked Agnetha from the lounge doorway.

"It's special," his mother told him. "Her first taste of pageantry."

"And hysteria," said James, looking at the cheering for the camera as people waved flags behind the presenter. "You never let me do anything when I was thirteen. Except homework."

"Ah," said his mother, "those were the days." James reckoned it was her policy to ignore accusations. "She won't get anywhere near the palace. People have been camping out for days. But it'll be an experience."

Agnetha looked at her watch and said she'd promised to take the bread rolls round. "I need to be back for eleven when Catherine arrives with her father."

"Have we got guests?" asked James. He knew it sounded like accusation number two but it wouldn't surprise him to find that his parents had invited all kinds of people he'd never met.

His mother smiled, tapped his head lightly and shook her head.

"No, James, I was referring to Kate Middleton arriving at Westminster Abbey. But you do remember that there's a street party later? Daph and Joel and the team must be setting up already."

She said she'd see him soon. When he heard her upstairs, saying goodbye to his dad, he hoped a kiss from a Swedish blonde might take Stephen's mind off the state of the shower. Olly liked to refer to James's parents as "loved up". Faith said they were "so embarrassing". It was hard to imagine anyone ever being all over Eleanor, or her being all over anyone. But he was sure lads like Jack or Guy would have handled it totally differently. With confidence. A casual, take-it-or-leave-it charm.

Well, Eleanor had left it, like half the salad. He told himself he had too (but not a trace of food). Sitting down on the sofa with his cereal, James couldn't find the remote, which Faith had a way of hiding. He felt too exhausted to change the channel. Ambushed. He'd woken up to a normal day and found this one was breaking all the rules and dictating all the terms – just like Eleanor would have tried to do, if he'd let her.

Had anyone considered the possibility of Wills or Kate finding an exit before they reached the Abbey?

Sue Hampton

TWO

Hema hadn't expected this. On the tube platform there was a people jam, thicker than any football crowd – but with fewer beer bellies, less nylon and a lot more smiles. Anant took her hand, but not gently. It felt more like a warning by a cross father who wanted to make sure a child didn't think about wandering off. As if she could move!

Pressed against her was one of those obese people she kept seeing on the TV news. Hema always pitied them, because although they were headless, they must recognise their clothes and shoes and feel so disrespected, as if millions of fingers were pointing at them and wagging. Averting her eyes from the belly, she gave its owner an understanding smile.

Anant frowned as if she'd just winked at some David Beckham lookalike. He wasn't normally quite so grumpy, but then she didn't usually insist and get her way. Now that he'd been proved right about the *"mayhem"* and things really did seem to be *"insane"* she didn't hold out much hope that the good humour in the April air might prove catching. Everyone else wedged on the platform seemed to be talking and laughing with complete strangers. Sometimes Hema thought London must be full of nicer boyfriends than hers.

"Please," she'd begged him the night before. "It's a historical event."

"Not yet," he said. "It's still in the future."

Hema was used to his pickiness but she often wondered how he'd react if she corrected him about his

English. Then he almost smiled, and she could see he thought he'd been smart. Was that what it was about – being cleverer than her? Because she didn't mind either way, preferring kindness and affection, but Anant was competitive and proud of it. It was what her father liked about him. It meant he'd succeed in the world.

As a train slowed to a stop, Anant's compact body tensed. The two of them were getting on; they had some kind of priority. He drilled and wormed, making space where there was none. Hema was pulled, apologising, through and in. The doors closed and dozens of the others were left behind, but some were so happy just to be part of the big day that they waved them off, and a couple of lads did it royal-style, with a slow twist of the hand, their chins high.

Why can't you be like them? thought Hema, but Anant's mood had lifted now.

"You're hopeless," he said, smiling. "You'd be stuck there all day."

She didn't reply. They were standing near the door but closer to elbows, backpacks and breath. Hema traced the filtering perfume, which was peppery, to a spreading middle-aged woman in a Union Jack dress and a wide-brimmed hat. The woman smiled at her. But why? Was it sympathy? Anant was Hema's first boyfriend and after two months the novelty of holding hands, and having someone to go to the cinema with, was wearing thin. Especially as he chose the films.

"Where are you heading for, then?" asked a man with a battered old top hat and sweat trickling down from it, plastering strands of black hair at the edge.

He was her dad's age at least. Hema didn't think Anant would like her being asked, but he'd like her answering even less.

18

"As close as we can get," she said, doubtfully. "Maybe just the screen in Hyde Park."

"Sounds like a plan," he said, as if he didn't have one either.

Hema thought the Union Jack woman must be his wife, because otherwise he'd be backing away from her rather large chest as it tilted towards him.

"Any wedding plans yourselves?" asked the woman, and winked. Her full mouth was outlined in dark, purplish red and the lips that swelled in between were day-glow cerise.

"You can't ask that!" Top Hat protested, but he grinned at her, and back at them, as if to say, *What is she like?*

"I'm only sixteen," said Hema, before Anant could say anything rude. "I've got exams ahead."

"That's it, love," said the woman. "Put your education first. That's what I should have done."

"Do you mind!" cried Top Hat.

"I'd still have married you, bozo! But I might not be working on a till for peanuts."

She said her name was Rita and he was Dan. Hema liked them, and the way they seemed to enjoy still being together, but she could almost feel Anant prickle.

"You working yet?" Dan asked him.

"I'm studying for A Levels," he said. Hema thought he felt confident that Dan wouldn't know how to spell his subjects. "Philosophy, Economics, Maths and Politics."

Show-off, thought Hema, but Dan was happy to look impressed. Rita told her Dan was a hard worker too.

They stopped at the next station but only one man left the carriage, with some difficulty. A few managed to edge in somehow. Dan said they must have S.A.S. training and most people allowed themselves a chuckle. Apart from Anant.

"Good to see everyone coming together," Dan said, eyes moving in a way body parts couldn't.

Hema understood. He meant race. Ethnic mix. She hoped Anant wasn't going to take it badly because it was meant to be positive and she sometimes felt like telling him people like these couldn't help being white.

"Yes, there are people here of all ages," she said, and looked away.

"We've come from the States," chipped in a sporty-looking woman in shades. "Oregon."

As she started to tell everyone how much interest there was in the event *"back home"*, Anant muttered in Hema's ear, "Not Oregon. Arrogant."

Hema shrugged. He was like a prosecuting attorney who accused people with no evidence and told the judge, *"Well, it's obvious!"*

Tourists were declaring themselves: China, Japan, Norway and Germany.

"Of course," said one woman with a Dutch accent, "we're here for Diana." There were wordless sounds of assent.

Anant leaned and whispered, "Will you tell her she's dead or shall I?"

Hema didn't smile. It wasn't funny and death bothered her. It was like an ornament that had always been on a shelf but she'd never really seen it, picked it up and dusted it off. And then someone gave it a name and now she saw it every day, and the rest of the room went out of focus around it. Her grandmother was gone. It was what grandmothers did and she couldn't talk to her friends about how much it hurt.

She didn't tell them where she met Anant, either – at the widow's house after a different funeral.

Not long after her grandmother's in Mauritius, this one had been at the nearest Methodist church in Brixton. It was where she once did Grade One Tap and Modern in the hall, and Hema remembered more about those moves, and the tinny backing tracks, than she remembered about the man her father now called "*the deceased.*"

She asked why she had to go. Who was he again? Even at the time she suspected her parents of knowing there would be young men in suits: businessmen, and businessmen-to-be. Contacts and clients her father needed to cultivate, some of them with sons. Her mother Celeste insisted that she must remember the dead man and how nice he'd been to her.

"You met him at that function in the town hall. He gave you sweets," said Celeste, as Hema made up a bed for her on the sofa.

Celeste wasn't well enough for ceremonies, and their neighbour, Shireen, arrived to keep her company. That meant two of them to inspect Hema before she left, and exchange glances. She wore a charcoal dress because her hair and shoes were black enough. Celeste wasn't sure it would do.

"I don't want to go as a Goth," objected Hema, from the door.

But she had to admit that deepest black suited Anant: a crisp suit, his gel gleaming, his shirt a bright white. He looked brand new and scented. Hema's father, Louis, who had a dry cleaning shop, was impressed.

"Devout too," he told her.

Her look meant *what?* And *how?*

Hema's father had been born to a Catholic family in Mauritius, but now he liked to say his religion was tolerance. Hema knew he approved piety whether it was Muslim or Christian, Jewish or Hindu. But had he really kept his eyes open during prayers to check on Anant?

In the dead man's lounge, Louis found someone to introduce them.

"A very good girl," he told Anant and his parents.

Hema couldn't glare. Instead she fixed her gaze on an ornate clock on the wall ahead. Her father wouldn't understand how humiliated she felt, how small and mislabelled. Not because she didn't want to be good, but because of what they'd think it meant. There were plenty of English words that could make a girl like her *"good"* for men who wanted the kind of wife she wouldn't be. Words like *submissive. Subservient. Doormat.*

Hema preferred a more modern word: *feisty.* But it was harder to earn than *"good"*.

Louis was an excitable party guest. Hema was used to him talking about moving to Dublin or Paris, but over a plate of cheeses, onion bhaji, felafel and tabbouleh he told Anant he was considering semi- retirement by the Kent or Sussex coast.

"I see myself running a modest B and B, you know, Anant. Traditional and homely. Proper English food".

Hema was astonished. The smell of fried egg made her nauseous and she liked Brixton most of the time.

Later, back home, Hema complained to her mother about her father's announcements to strangers.

"I thought he was going to broadcast my bra size!"

Then she tried not to blush because that, unlike her mother's, was small.

But Celeste only wanted to know about Anant. Leaning for the laptop, Celeste, whose grandfather had been born in Antigua, looked up Ugandan Asians and the expulsion by Amin, before Googling the name Anant. Excited, she found a whole list of *"eminent medics and scientists."*

"Mother," said Hema, "try tapping in feminism."

Hema knew her mother loved romance more than any other idea. And since she'd been off work, she'd become emotionally attached to the TV itself, as if the daytime presenters took the place of the colleagues she didn't see.

Today Hema had left her more upright on the sofa, with no bedcover and no Shireen, who had camped overnight on Clapham Common. Celeste would have loved to be there, and knew the timetable of events off by heart. But Louis had been persuaded to close the shop and share the day, the bubbly, and all the food his wife had found the stamina to make. Hema was sure her mother would be as happy as she'd decided to be. Much happier already, with her scars and her stiffness, painkillers and live-in slippers, than Hema expected to feel all day – with or without the highlight Celeste was counting on: a balcony kiss.

Hema thought it must be horrible to know the nation was waiting for that. Such a private thing. Life might not be perfect but she had no wish to be Kate, and give up a real life, and her real self, to perform on a global stage.

She wondered how many people in London today felt pity, and whether the answer made her as strange as she sometimes suspected.

Sue Hampton

THREE

Olly was at the front door, scruffy as usual. For a second James wondered whether he'd found out somehow about the date with Eleanor. Olly would be merciless, using it as material like the captains on *Have I Got News For You?* But there was no giveaway glint in his friend's eyes. Like the buttercups they hadn't fully opened yet.

"Olly Jordan?" Eleanor had echoed, when James mentioned him the night before. "First time I saw him from behind I thought he was Year Seven, full name Olivia."

"With that walk?" would have been one reply. Olly strode like a hill farmer in boots.

"With that face?" would have been another. Olly had the features of a still-curious thirty-year-old on top of that (fairly) short body.

"He's a mate," he could have said, as if that meant a full stop. Or, *"He's a great dancer,"* but she wouldn't believe that. And Olly's dancing, being untaught, resisted definition. Like other natural wonders, it had to be seen.

"You should hear what he says about you," he countered instead, and somehow, without intending, got the tone so ambiguous that Eleanor faltered. Couldn't read it. And didn't like it.

What followed was the longest silence yet.

This morning Olly's long hair was hanging – no intervention – which was apparently what Olly wanted to do at James's house. He said he had nothing particular to do except revision, and he didn't see why he should do that on a public holiday.

"You're not watching, are you?" he asked.

"Nah," said James.

It wasn't strictly true. He knew more about the dress the bride might be wearing than some of the clothes in his own wardrobe, and could probably have related the story of one family's rise from coal mines to Palace if it came up as an exam question.

James needed diversionary tactics.

"Did you sleep in those clothes?" he asked. Olly had been looking more like a homeless person since his mum said he was old enough to do his own ironing.

"Cup of tea'd be nice," he said.

As he followed James through to the kitchen, Olly said that in his house the wedding might lead to a (second) divorce. His step-dad, who was a company director, was also ex-Socialist Worker and wanted to go to the Republican street party that had been in the news. But his mum had decided at the last minute to stay home and watch the coverage after all.

Olly's shoulders hunched up and his face contracted in mystification. "She isn't even a monarchist."

"My dad says supporting a monarchy is an untenable position," said James, "like slavery."

"Right," said Olly. He paused. "Nine ten what?"

"Untenable! A position you can't hold. Morally."

"Ah," said Olly. "Yeah. Not in the twenty-first century."

"You know people still have to stop eating when the Queen puts down her knife and fork and leave the rest on their plates?"

"You're kidding!"

James grinned. If Olly hadn't been anti-monarchy before, he would be now. James had never seen him leave as much as a smear of food on any plate. "Toast?"

It was as they waited for the toaster to deliver that Olly heard cheering in the lounge. James pretended he hadn't.

"Who's watching?" Olly asked. "Sprite? Where is that sister of yours? She hasn't tried to attack me for months."

James tried the sheepish smile that worked with his mum. "You got me," he mumbled. "Faith's out, up in town. I got drawn in somehow."

Olly's mouth stretched wide and he let a tight, dry noise from the back of his throat. "Untenable position?" he triumphed.

"All right!" said James, hand on the lever of the toaster. "Do you want breakfast or not? There's a café round the corner if you've got a tenner on you."

"Gotcha or what!" continued Olly, still amused.

James knew this story was going to run and run, like the Big News itself. Not that Olly, who went to the nearest grammar, had much contact with James's friends from school, some of whom were boarders with homes in Norfolk or Liverpool, Tanzania or Shanghai. James expected most people in his year would be taking a break from Keats, erosion and the Peasants' Revolt to wave flags and thrust their phones into spaces between heads. Any minute now they'd be tweeting that they snapped the backside of a guardsman's horse or climbed a tree for an aerial view of Camilla's hat.

Olly had no idea there was a street party until James told him.

"A real one? Not an ironic one to make a point?"

"I suppose it makes a point," said James. "A few, probably. But don't ask Faith what they are. She just likes overacting in dramas. Real ones."

He didn't admit that Faith seemed to have a crush on Prince Harry because that was worrying on more than one level and Olly might suggest others that he hadn't thought of.

They found themselves wandering into the lounge, where the TV showed streets around the country being dressed and equipped for parties.

"Are we having salsa dancing at ours?" asked Olly, soggy cornflakes escaping between milky lips and being knuckled back as he talked.

"You'll have to ask my mum. Apparently she's in charge of rolls."

"I bet your mum can dance salsa."

"She's from Stockholm, not South America!"

High Streets and avenues made way for the Mall as the Queen and Duke of Edinburgh left Buckingham Palace.

"If I was the producer," said Olly, "I'd mike up the Duke and wait all of two seconds for him to open his mouth and put his foot in it."

"She was beautiful, you know," said James, looking at the Queen.

Olly stared.

"That's a tenable position," said James, "backed up by photographic evidence."

Olly seemed unconvinced. The bridesmaids and pages were on camera now, leaving the hotel, just as James looked round to see both his parents appear in the doorway and look straight past them to the screen. His father was carrying a bottle and glasses.

"Oh, bless!" said Agnetha. "Poor little scraps."

"We're fine, Mum," said James, "and Olly can't help being short."

"Hi, Olly. Ignore James."

"Standard practice."

The two friends sat on the other sofa and James's dad poured champagne.

"Have you changed position recently, Mr Allnutt?" asked Olly innocently. He gasped when James kicked his ankle.

"Just getting comfortable, Olly," said Stephen. "I take it you won't say no to a drop of bubbly?"

Olly sat forward, grinning, and admitted he'd never had any, because of the bubbles, but he'd try holding his nose to stop them getting in.

"What about the party?" asked James, accepting a glass and taking a first sip.

"That's afterwards," said Agnetha. "Lunch, if the rain holds off. A couple of husbands are buttering as we speak."

"I'm sure they'd appreciate help, lads," said Stephen, "if you don't want to watch."

"You're all right," said James. "Thanks, Dad."

On the coffee table was a ring binder and pen. Noticed only by Olly, James devoted a page each to some key words, carefully spelt.

"Dad," he called, and when his father glanced over, held up the notebook: DEMOCRACY? He tore away the first page so that his father could see PUBLIC MONEY! followed by EQUALITY?

"Oh, very Dylan," said Stephen, but his eyes were soon back on Kate, soon to be Princess Catherine, off to the Abbey in a Rolls Royce.

"Beautiful dress," murmured Agnetha.

"She looks stunning," said Stephen, "just like you were." She turned, grinning. "Are!"

They kissed and chinked champagne flutes. Olly almost sprayed bubbles through his nose. James gave him a look that meant, *What can I say?*

"There are nibbles in the kitchen, boys," said Agnetha distractedly, "if you want to bring them in, or take some upstairs…"

In the kitchen Olly looked entertained. "We'd better knock before we go back in again."

James didn't say it was better than divorce. He felt a kind of pride mixed in with the embarrassment, but it was more than that. His mum and dad were happy. They loved each other still. So there was some point in marriage – or could be, if you got lucky.

He supposed that technically he shouldn't have been at his parents' wedding. He wasn't sure how much he remembered and how much he'd just imagined because he'd heard the story – mainly his brother's version. Phil was at uni now, doing French, (and might be the only member of the family standing up for principles like *egalité*, even if he was doing it horizontally, in bed) but at the time, he'd been seven. James was three.

Apparently, they'd woken up one morning to find their parents looking excited, and been told they had to have their hair washed, even before breakfast. Phil refused at first to wear his school trousers. But the only photograph that existed (which they asked some official to take outside the Registry Office) showed him looking sorry he'd given in. And James was wearing soft, jogging-type elasticated pull-ons that bulged at the knees because he lived in them. Plus a shirt with a little bow tie that he kept trying to pull off, but only pinged. Which hurt more when Phil did it.

Eventually Agnetha came downstairs in a dark red dress and stepped into some high black heels. No tights, because James always stroked those when she wore them, but when he checked with his fingers, her legs were bare.

"We're going to get married," she told them, and the story went that James clapped and jumped. Phil asked why – and whether they'd be back in time for some cartoon programme that made him bounce on the sofa.

There was no church. No relatives either, because Agnetha's parents were in Sweden so it didn't seem fair to ask Stephen's. And besides, it was last minute, an idea that sneaked up on them.

Faith loved the story and was really sick that she'd missed it. James was sure she embellished it for all her friends. But she also intended to have six bridesmaids and a veil and train and do it in style when her turn came. He wondered where she'd got to and imagined her being even sicker if she missed this wedding too.

James thought they'd better take the tortilla chips through while there was still some dip in the pots because a large amount clung to Olly's upper lip.

Someone seemed to have planted trees in Westminster Abbey.

"It's a bit more elaborate than ours," said Agnetha, holding Stephen's hand.

"Bet they'd rather be doing it our way," he said.

Cue for another kiss to make Olly's eyes bulge and lift to the ceiling.

The clouds above Hyde Park were streaky grey as Anant and Hema made their way in, slowly. Anant had said they wouldn't be able to get inside at all because it was full up, and didn't seem pleased to be wrong.

"It's going to rain," he said.

"You keep saying that," Hema murmured. "I think it's brightening up."

Other people thought so too. There was hardly an umbrella or kagoule in sight, but plenty of red, white and blue. Hema felt smaller than usual, like a child in the cinema with adult heads and shoulders breaking up her view. But here there were three screens, so tall that a Routemaster bus couldn't block them. Behind them rose enormous trees that must have seen other crowds, celebrating, demonstrating. Hema had never been in such a crowd, and when she'd seen footage of the student protests on the streets a few months earlier, she'd felt glad not to be there in the midst of something so frightening, with its own life that wasn't quite human, a shapeless, fluid mass. Hema hated chanting when it was a threat, each word hurled like a stone.

She'd stopped watching the news now because of Libya, and she didn't dare talk to Anant about that. He backed NATO but Hema didn't understand why no one had learned from Iraq.

There was no anger in Hyde Park. No sun, either, but Hema wished Anant would enjoy what everyone else would call a great atmosphere. On screen things were happening. The bride was leaving her hotel and cheers greeted her, or her dress, or both. Hema's head tilted up enough to see, but Anant was pulling at her arm, determined to get nearer.

"No," she protested. "I don't want to move. I'll miss it. We're fine here."

"Come on!"

"These people have been here hours. You can't push your way to the front. It'd be over by the time you got there, anyway."

"We might as well be at home watching properly."

Hema didn't answer this time. She just watched the Rolls Royce making its way to Westminster Abbey.

"She's very pretty," she said, and remembered that there was a Kate doll. Now they would sell a miniature of the dress for it. She didn't share thoughts like those with Anant, but she knew that she would have begged her mother for that doll if she'd been eight instead of sixteen.

A week earlier Celeste was knitting the Royal Family and a Corgi too. She showed Hema the cardboard balcony and the wire that would help the woollen figures to raise a hand to the crowd.

"I should have taught you to knit," she said. "You could have helped me finish in time."

"For what?" asked Hema, supposing the figures would decorate the table like the singing, dancing Santa that came out of the cupboard every Christmas. "I wouldn't want to spoil your fun."

"Shireen is going to do Charles," her mother said, "and Camilla in pink. But I told her to let me sew the smiles on. You need a steady hand for that."

"Camilla won't wear pink," said Hema, but her mother's laugh meant she was being ridiculous.

"You've got inside information on that, have you? Been ringing Clarence House to offer fashion advice?"

For days the project kept her mother cheerful. Celeste couldn't have knitted with any more commitment if a baby had been due any minute. Then, when the family was finished, smiling and speared through with wire, Louis took them for the window of the dry cleaner's, promising to remember instructions about how they should be arranged. And Shireen drove Celeste round an hour later so they could inspect the display to make sure he hadn't put the Corgi between bride and groom, and Camilla's waving arm didn't look as if it was slapping Charles in the face.

Every day since, Celeste had asked Louis whether any customers had made appreciative comments. Every day he said they had, and quoted them, which meant Celeste had to ring Shireen to repeat the observations, decorated a little like the knitted faces. Hema suspected Louis of inventing at least a few of them.

Now, as Westminster Abbey filled the screen, Hema's mouth opened at the sight of Prince William, waiting for his bride. Not in Air Force blue, as the knitting pattern dictated, but red! Imagining Celeste's horror, she hoped the whole day wasn't ruined. Especially since the camera showed that Camilla was not, in fact, in pink, and had a hat larger than anyone might have imagined.

Looking at the backs and necks in front of her, Hema realised that she knew these people as well as she knew Anant. She remembered hearing that in a crowd you could feel truly lonely. She should have come with her friends.

"Good figure," said Anant, meaning Pippa Middleton, whose backside was slinkily curved. Hema considered him rude, and had once objected when he'd admired Tess Daly's legs on *Strictly*, but he'd told her it was just the same as appreciating a good song or good painting.

She didn't react, in case he expected her to.

When the camera picked up David Beckham a few seconds later, she said, "Good body," and he barked, "What?" but she only murmured, "Nothing."

The next celebrities on screen were Elton John and David Furnish. Hema liked them, and their baby, and the way they'd planned it so that no one knew which one of them was the biological father. She knew what Anant thought, but the word he used shocked her.

What's *queer*, she thought, is your attitude, which is out of step with twenty-first century thinking. If anything's sad it's your tough guy act.

The bride arrived and the crowd in the park became almost rapturous, enjoying whatever it was that Harry reported to his brother. Around her, Hema heard a kind of Chinese whispers as people attempted to lip read. Why did everyone like a naughty boy better than a good one?

The train was being adjusted. Hema remembered that Princess Diana had felt like a lamb to the slaughter but this bride was meant to be savvy, with 'life experience'. Hema wondered how much of that she would have acquired, herself, over the next twelve years. Her parents would expect her to be a mother of three by then, and make up for their own lack of sons. Would the royal couple feel under even greater obligation to produce a boy? Or had Diana changed that too? Would a beautiful daughter for the front pages be better for the economy?

As William smiled at Kate Middleton, Hema smiled too, because for now at least, he loved her.

Anant had never looked at her like that. She had no idea what she was doing with him, and no idea how to walk away.

FOUR

Agnetha and Stephen kissed again as the royal couple met at the altar. James put a hand over his eyes. Olly squirmed.

"Is this in Latin?" Olly asked two minutes later.

"Is there much more?" came soon afterwards.

When James suggested checking out the street party, his parents didn't look too sad to see them go.

Outside, Olly pulled up his hood and James pretended he wasn't cold in his T-shirt. They both lived at the same, cheaper end, which was nearest to a regular street, the sort with traffic. But further along, after the road curved around, it was tucked away from the rest of the neighbourhood like a very long, tree-lined drive to a health spa.

James guessed that the houses, whether Georgian or Sixties multi-level experiments, were mostly mansions, with gardens that almost hid them, and security gates like electronic drawbridges. He'd recognise a few of the cars they opened to admit, but the only people he knew by sight were the dog walkers who acknowledged him with an, *"Evening,"* as he walked back from Olly's place some nights. It might not be too much of a trek from the High Street or the tube but it wasn't what he'd call a community.

At the far end, where the cul-de-sac led only to a wooded area fronted by laurels, paeonies and rhododendron bushes, the bunting was flapping already, as middle-aged residents carried garden chairs to place around the trestle tables. Union Jack tablecloths had to be pinned down with picnic plates on top of the paper.

A silvery ghetto-blaster added the cathedral choir to the sounds of furniture removal and the crackle of the first flames on a row of top-of-the range barbecues. A large man in an England apron with three shiny lions rampant across his chest watched and poked, placing firelighters and wiping his forehead.

"Olly," called Joel. "James, is it? Come to help?"

They didn't actually answer but were directed towards "Catering manager! Otherwise known as commanding officer. Or wife!" Under cover of a crush of choirboy voices gathering up to an angelic height, Olly murmured that Joel used to be some sort of General, Brigadier or Field Marshal who'd probably expected an invitation to the Abbey.

Daph, who was angular and perfumed, appeared to be wearing a tiara.

"Boys! Bravo! Bravo!" she cried, and gave them orders to carry a tea urn, "carefully as a coffin!"

James and Olly chose to imagine it was a grand piano on a stairway. Olly supplied the accidental chords complete with pedal effect simulated through the nose.

Then they chose balloons over buttering, sitting on one of the ornate, scroll-legged seats being produced from back gardens.

"Tame or what?" said Olly, glancing around them.

"Where are the sounds of Rio?" asked James, hand to one ear.

Olly tied a balloon and headed it upwards, beckoning it down impatiently and then managing to miss it. Then just as James knotted his first, Olly pierced it with a sharp fingernail.

James shoved him so hard that he fell into his own balloon, squashing it until that one burst too.

"Steady, lads," called the brigadier.

"It's just James," said Olly. "Flatulence problem." He used a hand to waft the problem away. "Eleanor Langridge was complaining," he added quietly, just for James. "You'll need manners if you want to take Eleanor out."

James frowned. She had spoken to Olly? Why? How? Was this Facebook or was Olly tweeting now? And what had she said?

"I don't, thanks," he said. "Want to take her out. I'd rather spend an evening with a porcupine."

"Ouch!" said Olly, mis-hitting a balloon with his head. Hairs lifted with static. "Why ask her then? Why mess her about?"

James was incredulous. What was going on?

"Mess her about!"

He tried to punch the balloon but missed. Olly pulled an annoying face.

"That's what I said," he said, and it wasn't provocative. It was hard-line.

"You want to get your information straight," James muttered, "before you go wading in."

He couldn't remember anything like this before. There was enough needle in the air to get every balloon popping.

"She's vulnerable," said Olly, accusingly.

"Eleanor Langridge!"

"Yes, in fact, but you didn't bother to find that out."

"What's the agenda, Olly? You got a crush?"

Maybe outsiders wouldn't pick it up, the serrated edge. Maybe to the Brigadier and the others it sounded like the usual lad banter. James knew it was different and he felt hurt, confused, astounded.

There was a sound from a back pocket that slung down low beneath Olly's bottom. He pulled it out and put it to his ear and James could tell straight away that it wasn't a tactic. He walked away, his back to James.

Then Olly turned, pulled in his mouth and let it drop again before he mouthed, "Got to go," and asked, "Which hospital, Mum?" as he walked away, then started to run. "I want to see him anyway!"

James had heard enough to explain. "I think his granddad's had a heart attack," he said, and reminded himself, not for the first time, never to joke around with the death word.

"Still *death in Sweden?*" he asked his dad, seven years earlier, when his mum didn't come to pick him up from primary school because she was too upset.

It was his father's phrase, the one he mouthed or whispered through those months, whenever Agnetha hadn't cooked supper, or didn't get up to make breakfast. When she'd forgotten to wash his games kit and when, just once or twice, he waited in bed but she never came to kiss him goodnight. The months, which were longer than usual, began with a phone call from Stockholm.

"Death is bad enough," said Stephen, the night it began, when she flew out after the call. "But your auntie was thirty-nine. And you know she was more than a sister."

They were twins. Soul-mates, Agnetha said.

James was about to be nine, and the rock climbing party was all booked. He tried not to ask what would happen to his birthday but it was hard not to wonder.

Days after she'd gone, he could still hear his mother trying to breathe as she clung to his dad. Picturing his cousins in Sweden, he could only see toddlers playing with push-along jeeps and a glove puppet of a dragon, but he knew Ingmar was at school now and probably didn't cry any more when he tripped over the root of a tree. This would be a different kind of sobbing.

Agnetha was in Stockholm for ten days and Faith woke him with nightmares. One night he heard her crying quietly and went to her room. At first he wondered whether she had a crowd of teddies in bed with her, bulging out a mound alongside.

"It's all right," he told her. "It's not our mum who's dead."

"I know," she retorted, wiping her nose with her wrist. "I'm not stupid. But she's lost half her heart. She told Dad."

She marched off to the bathroom and he lifted the duvet to find Agnetha's dressing gown bundled and warm on the sheet.

When they met their mother from the airport she looked so different that for a second James thought it was the wrong twin. The bones in her face stuck out under her eyes where the skin was darker, and her hair was pulled away in a pony tail that made her forehead look taut and pale.

She brought back a photo of his auntie laughing, one son on each side.

Walking back to his own house with a hasty, "See you later," James realised the photograph of the twin blondes must still be on the shelf in the lounge, but he'd stopped seeing it. He found the house silent, and his father washing the champagne glasses.

"Mum's been crying," Stephen told him. "Diana and the princes – echoes, you know? Your cousins won't have a mum at their weddings either."

"Ah," said James.

He remembered Agnetha saying that the tragic princess was still a trigger or a symbol for some of the clients who came for therapy, because they identified or projected in some way. He hadn't understood that she shared it too – with a few million others. But of course she did. Still *death in Sweden*.

"We might not be partying straight away," Stephen told him. "Where's Olly?"

James explained. His father sighed and shook his head. "Happy days are always sad for someone."

"Yeah, but why is it happy?" asked James. "For anyone but them, I mean. What makes the population behave like we've won the World Cup?"

"Your mother can give you the psychology. I don't really get it either. I just decided to go with it." His father hung up the tea towel and studied the contents of the open box of chocolates on the worktop. "Help yourself," he told James. "We've left you some good ones."

When it came to chocolate, James could pick with his eyes shut.

"So as a society we make out we're spiky peanut brittles," he said, teeth clogged with toffee and his diction less than clear, "but given half a chance we become heart-shaped strawberry crèmes."

His father didn't catch his meaning but before he could ask him to repeat his theory with less suck and chew, Agnetha was running down the stairs calling his name. James heard them in the hallway.

"I called Faith's phone and someone switched it off. It wasn't her."

"I expect it was. She probably knocked it off by mistake. Or there's so much screaming she decided to turn off because she couldn't hear a word."

"She'd shout above it, wouldn't she, to tell me she's all right – if she is all right."

James could hear that his mother, who was usually calm and almost always drew the most positive conclusion, was being reactive for once. His dad pointed out that it was probably the safest day of the year to be out in central London.

James pushed the door to join them.

"She's with her friends," he said, although he couldn't remember which ones they were and none of them seemed particularly stable to him. They all squealed and hugged when they greeted each other, as if they hadn't met for years.

"Unless they've got separated," said Agnetha, "and she can't find them because she's lost her phone."

James thought it was more likely that Faith had just forgotten the parents who might worry, or, having rushed off without charging her battery, was leaving her phone at the bottom of her bag.

Agnetha looked in her diary for phone numbers of the parents concerned, but the names she remembered were new. She realised she'd never had their contact details.

"Even if she was in trouble," James said, regretting the word, "which is very unlikely, she's in the best place. Someone will help."

Picturing Faith in the crowd, cut off from her friends and possibly phoneless one way or another, he felt unexpectedly protective. Could someone have stolen her bag? He didn't want to think of that. She was too young to be stranded, scared and helpless, with no ticket home.

But his father was agreeing with his positive spin. "She won't have to go far to ask a policeman," added Stephen with a smile.

James wondered whether his parents had both dismissed the same mental picture, but no one was admitting to it. He remembered statistical probability. Besides, Faith had initiative. She'd wanted to prove her independence and now she'd have the chance.

Agnetha had a therapist's voice for her answer machine and James knew she was trying to find it, along with the reassuring smile. She tapped in Faith's number again, loosening her shoulders and trying to smile.

"No answer," she said, eventually.

"I predict," added Stephen, "that she'll come home covered in anti-climb paint, exhausted and a little bit grumpy."

"Mm," said Agnetha, and he kissed her forehead and told her to get ready for the party.

"You coming, James?" asked Stephen. "Is it marginally more attractive than revision?"

James made a show of considering. "Hard to call," he said.

"Would you stay, love?" asked his mother, stopping at the top of the stairs. "In case Faith calls the house phone. I know the chances are there's no problem at all but..."

"Sure."

"You don't mind?"

James shook his head and lifted his eyebrows. "Go party," he said.

At the end of the service there was clapping and cheering. Twelve fifteen. The carriage they called the State Landau began to take the couple to the palace and Hema wished she was there, waiting to wave, like the crowds chanting, "We want Kate" on the Mall.

"Shall we move?" she asked Anant. "See it for ourselves? It's not far."

Anant's face twisted up; he didn't look handsome at all. "Are you crazy? You heard what they said – half a million people on the Mall."

Am I crazy, thought Hema, to be wasting time with you?

"We could make it half a million and two?" she muttered but it was lost in crowd reaction to looks and waves from the royal couple. Some of those in the park waved back.

"Have you had enough?" he asked. "Happy now?"

"You want to go home? It's only just starting..."

"It just finished!"

"But they'll come out on the balcony," said Hema, thinking of the woollen figures, "for a kiss."

"Yes, a timed kiss, for the cameras. It's been scheduled."

She shrugged. "That doesn't mean it's not genuine."

"You don't know it is." He allowed himself a smile but today she didn't like it. "I can give you a real kiss any time you like."

Hema ignored that. Anant's kisses had lost their novelty value and were less romantic than the earliest

45

used to be, her first. Now they felt hard sometimes, as if he was angry with her – for something she'd done, or wouldn't do.

"Can't we just stay until they come out on the balcony? It's only another hour."

"I know when it is," he said. "I'm hungry. We can go back and watch it at mine."

As if his parents rented space in a house he owned.

"No, thanks," she said, amazed at herself. "We might not get back in time, and anyway, it wouldn't be the same."

She reminded him that she had brought packed lunch in a tub but he said he didn't like her mother's idea of Indian food.

Hema frowned. What did that mean?

"You don't come from India either," she muttered. She told herself not to be over-sensitive but it felt too late to stop now.

"Look," he said, "I don't want to stay here until it finally rains," he said, "just to see a kiss on a big screen that I could see on a smaller one – if I wanted to see it at all. And I don't want to sit on the grass and eat cold, greasy food that makes my eyes water. I was only humouring you in the first place."

"You don't need to humour me if it makes you so..." Hema stopped. Was there such a word as bad-humoured? "I'd rather have stayed at home."

"Ha! There I concur!"

He sounded like a lawyer already, she thought, but here, amidst the Union Jack hats and seaside mood, it was so ridiculous that she half-expected eavesdroppers to laugh out loud.

"So let's go," he added, and tried to grab her hand or arm, but she shrugged him off, turning her shoulder. "Come on! What's your problem?"

Hema knew the answer to that.

"You," she said, surprised to hear the word so clearly over everything else. He heard it too.

"What?"

It was quick and sharp enough for a bacon slicer and it pushed her on.

"You are. I don't want to be with you. So I'd prefer it if you went home and left me to be as crazy as I like."

His eyebrows slanted, his eyes narrow. Then he shook his head, and he almost looked amused.

"You're dumping me?"

"That's not the nicest word..."

"On Royal Wedding day?" He made a noise like a laugh that was also a huff, as he breathed air through his long nose. Strong, her father called it.

"I can't see what difference it makes what day it is..."

"You've been weird all day," he told her, sullen now.

"You've been... mean."

"Mean! Are we five years old?"

Hema looked up to the screen but he pulled her shoulder.

"No one dumps me."

Hema wrenched herself free. She felt as if he was like a prompt backstage, giving her cues, and the answers were there, ready, just waiting to be spoken.

"There's a first time for everything. Isn't that what you told me?"

"Bitch," he said, and she was glad to be in the crowd. Not on a street in darkness, just the two of them.

47

Anant pushed through and away. Hema felt the sting of fear. She didn't know him, what he might be capable of, whether pride would make him let go or cling on. She realised she might cry. Picturing her parents' astonishment and dismay, she imagined telling them it was a private matter before this new assertiveness slipped away like wedding fever.

"Are you all right, love?"

Hema had noticed the mother and daughter, Afro-Caribbean, one wide, one petite. One in a kind of smock that draped down like a tent from the bust, the other in stretchy Lycra with contours. It was the mother who asked but the daughter, who was probably twenty, looked down from the screen too.

"Best off without him," she told Hema.

"You told him good," said her mother.

"I didn't plan to," admitted Hema.

"You save yourself for someone with a bit of respect," added the daughter. "I'm Beatrice, like the princess."

"With the terrible hat," said her mother.

Hema knew they were being kind but she felt ashamed – of letting strangers know her personal business.

"I'm Hema," she mumbled, and longed for something big to happen on screen that would make these women, and anyone else who'd overheard her end her first relationship, delete and move on.

And there it was – the Queen herself, giving her verdict. *Awesome?* Had she been watching *The Simpsons*? In fact, it seemed that the word was *"amazing"*. There were more cheers and Hema looked away to the other side of the park, considering the chances of being able to work a way across. Of leaving the whole scene behind and being anonymous again.

She pulled the women a quick little smile and began to move, asking politely, then upping the volume, lifting her head in order to connect with the faces. Some made her a space. Some didn't seem to see or hear. Hema felt very small and strangely alone.

FIVE

"Extreme," Faith had said when they'd spilt out of the tube. It was one of her favourite words, and fitted all kinds of things including Olly Jordan's dancing and her parents' behaviour. James did an impression of her using it – too much. But she hadn't expected this. Even though she'd read on her new phone that at six a.m. the crowd behind the barriers had been fifteen deep, it wasn't until she saw the human blockage for herself that it seemed real.

"We should've brought sleeping bags last night," she told Ayesha then. "Or the night before."

"No way," said Ayesha, and patted her hair, which was piled up and pinned, tall as a busby. Dressed for some kind of award ceremony, Ayesha looked sixteen. But Faith couldn't see the structure holding all day with flags and elbows all around.

"It's hopeless," said Tash. "We won't see a thing."

On St James's Park there were stalls selling gin and tonic.

"Let's get one!" cried Ayesha.

"Don't be stupid," said Tash, who was looking sulky already, and at five foot two stood no chance, especially with Union Jack ribbons tied round wiry plaits.

"Moody," reacted Ayesha.

Faith might not have come along at all if she'd known that only the two of them would actually be present at the station. Faith felt like the average one in the middle –

between tall, sophisticated Ayesha and chunky Tash with her St Trinian's look, customised with a red heart on each cheek. The letters C and W were smudged now and the hearts were starting to fuzz away at the edges, but Tash was proud because the other painted faces all seemed to have Union Jacks.

"Little Miss Romantic," had been Ayesha's greeting, but she hadn't sounded impressed.

People were already up in trees and Faith had seen home-made periscopes. She realised the three of them were seriously under-prepared as well as forty-eight hours too late. And the scale of it all had been fun for five minutes, until the novelty started wearing away faster than Tash's face paint.

There was an argument about buying baked potatoes because Tash was hungry but Ayesha wasn't. Faith felt frustrated by the two of them. They were so easily distracted, as if there was no mission. But for Faith, now that they were there, and only half a million people away from the stage where the show would soon begin, it was obvious they should be taking action. Quickly, with some kind of purpose. Otherwise what was the point? Faith liked to have a point, even if it was to stay in bed and recover. And where James was concerned, she liked to make a point too, as often as possible – one that he couldn't smart-mouth back and overturn. Which was hard to do.

The best place they could find to stand, eventually, was about sixteen people back from the barrier and what Tash called miles away from the palace. An argument broke out, along the lines of *"Told you!"* and *"Not my fault!"* Then a text informed them that Lu, Fliss, Ruby, Xitong and Janis had a good view of the screen in Hyde Park.

Tash wanted to join them.

Ayesha said that was stupid.

Faith would have liked to slip away and abandon them both if she'd thought she had any hope of finding the others.

They heard the service on the loudspeakers and watched on their phones – although Tash had run out of battery, which meant sharing a tiny screen. Faith realised it would have to be hers, as the other two might soon object to breathing the same cubic metre of air.

In spite of the sun that appeared as Kate made it to the altar, Faith was too cold by then to have any hope of thawing out. Imagining the HD colour on the set in the lounge with shivery longing, she wondered whether James would be watching. He was way more fun than Ayesha and Tash.

"OMG! Bor-ing!" said Ayesha.

"No one asked you to come."

Faith couldn't even find out what her brother was doing because Tash was holding her phone as if it was a make-up mirror or lolly.

Then Ayesha mouthed, "Fit," and her eyes went into action. Faith realised she was flirting wordlessly with some Asian lads, two bodies to the right and three rows forward. It was quite a skill. Faith puffed out crossly.

"Pur-lease!" muttered Tash.

Some individual form of sign language seemed to be going on and Ayesha was enjoying the game so much that she'd stopped trying not to show it. Tash's face set grim around the hearts.

Then, just as music swelled in layers around them, Ayesha nodded towards Tash and Faith like a captain to privates in a war zone. She started to manoeuvre through, horizontally, without checking behind. The lads seemed to be edging backwards. Tash sighed noisily – but looked back to see a wave just for her. That was all it took! Tash thrust Faith's phone at her and followed – probably leaving traces of red on every jacket and shirt in her path.

Faith turned to watch, mouth hanging. Then she turned back. No way!

Faith did hear, "You coming, Faith?" but she didn't feel like answering, or moving either. They were so out of order! Because to go backwards seemed ridiculous. And because she didn't chase boys. They'd have to chase her and she couldn't promise it would get them anywhere if they did.

Instead Faith kept her head focused on the mini TV screen. Bristling. Seething. The words weren't strong enough! She rehearsed her account, key word *outrageous*. But she didn't really have a plan or an intention. When James called her stubborn she was proud. No giving in. No weakening. But when she did look round, all she could see was a glimpse of Ayesha's column of hair.

For a whole hymn Faith kept watching the service in the Abbey, and told herself she didn't care and she wasn't running – or rather, squeezing – to catch them up. Then she felt a pang of anxiety. And aloneness. And looked back, tiptoeing, leaning, but they'd gone.

All she could do was head back in the same direction, find a space somewhere and call Ayesha. If they didn't meet up they could identify a spot – somehow – and join up, lads or no lads. Couldn't they?

"No sense of direction," was what James told her. Or sometimes, "No sense!" But it couldn't be too hard to find someone with hair like Ayesha's. For a minute or two she excused herself politely through the crowd. For another five she was less apologetic, more assertive. She still couldn't see them.

Faith felt too cross to cry, even at failure. She'd given up their so-called vantage point, and for nothing. She couldn't be enjoying the ceremony any less if she'd been locked in the bathroom. And the only thing she could think to do was talk to James until she felt better.

Faith looked for her phone but it must be hiding amongst the tissues, gum, sunglasses and sun cream. The purse, keys, lip salve and mirror, juice carton and socks. And a small photo of James posing, which just fitted in one side pocket. Where was it? She rummaged again. Then she checked the back pocket of her jeans. Since a train ticket had fallen out of that pocket onto a disgusting toilet floor, she'd made a mental note not to trust it again. But had she reverted to old habits without thinking?

Faith never used her top jacket pocket because James said she could radiate her heart, but she patted it anyway. Thinking of James sent a wobble inside her nose down into her chest. Even if the phone was down on the ground – between feet, along with rucksacks and carrier bags and the odd discarded plastic bottle – it was lost anyway. In the absence of a loudhailer.

The royal couple were leaving the Abbey now. At last the show would be heading her way but now she wouldn't see as much as a horse's buttock.

Not that she cared about backsides – horses' or Pippa Middleton's. Or carriages or kisses. Faith wanted her phone.

For the first time it occurred to her that at home Agnetha might be worrying because she hadn't called or sent a text. And now that she couldn't, Faith was worried herself. She had no hope of finding anyone or anything: her phone, her so-called friends or a view through the crowd. And her way home alone? Could she manage that?

Faith knew she'd have to. Or she'd be giving James a story he could grin about whenever he wanted to remind her of the years between them. There were maps to look at, street signs, and people to ask.

She'd rather be home already, beating him with a cushion on the sofa that she sometimes thought was harder than he was. But she could do it. He'd be proud of her.

Looking back, Olly scowled at the hospital. He didn't like concrete or the way they made it hard to know where to go or what to do. The size and scale of it, most of all, so that the sick and dying people inside it were lost or hidden somewhere among the lift shafts and corridors where only technology could track them. If he asked anyone in uniform where his granddad was (his dead granddad) no one would know and even a name would mean next to nothing. And the living were just as anonymous as the dead.

"I want to see," he'd argued. "I won't see him again."

But he hadn't known what it meant. *Dead* was different on TV. The actors got up and lit fags or drank tea. His granddad was grey and stony and he could feel the chill without touching – just like when his hamster cooled and hardened in the cage. Olly knew people who'd lost grandparents, but not his. His was different. His was the most important person in his life – or used to be. Before Olly got too old to need an old man hanging round. Before his granddad got too old to keep up.

Olly watched the revolving doors, opening up wide enough for wheelchairs or trolleys. People on crutches, in nightwear or hospital gowns, were smoking outside. They overlooked the street where the healthy strolled free – but today the patients outnumbered them.

"Heinz, like the beans," his granddad would say, "but only half-baked."

When Olly was little, he didn't understand the joke. But he knew Heinz was more fun than your average granddad. Heinz said he had perfect timing because World War Two ended before he was eighteen so he never had to fight for Hitler.

"Tell me the story," he said to his mum on the way to the hospital, because he'd forgotten so much of it.

He knew his granddad came to England as a young man, with his mother and her new English husband, to start again and hope nobody minded their accents. Heinz had an average surname but he refused to become Joe or Fred. How old had he been? And how come Gerta had married a Brit from the Foreign Office anyway? As if it mattered now. But it did then, to an unusual kind of family.

"You remember," said his mother, eyes on the road ahead, sounding too weary to begin it.

"Didn't people do… you know… finger moustaches and Heil Hitler salutes?" asked Olly, illustrating. "I mean, wasn't it hard?"

His mother nodded. In the driver's mirror she looked pale and Olly thought she must be in shock. But Heinz was eighty-four and amazing. Had been. Heinz was dead.

Now a pale-faced, blotchy woman emerged from the hospital and took a burger box from a visitor who'd just arrived. The smell of onions and ketchup mingled with the cigarette smoke and the tang of city dirt. Olly looked at his watch. How long? They'd done the identification. It was a bit late to say goodbyes.

Olly used to wave goodbye to his parents when Heinz arrived to look after him.

"Now the fun starts!" said his granddad. Or, "What mischief shall we get up today?"

Olly remembered waking from naps as a toddler to the sound of Heinz vacuuming.

He remembered Heinz opening cans of alphabet spaghetti or meatballs in sauce and telling him, "Don't tell your mother."

He remembered Heinz getting cross with the pushchair when it had to be folded up quickly for the bus. Thanking the driver for waiting and telling him he'd go to heaven.

It was Heinz who taught him to swim and ride a bike and have fun through the divorce. How to play Cheat and Patience and Whist as well as Snap. Whether paw prints round the bin store had been left by a stray dog or urban fox. How to wire up a plug, fold an origami dove and make an omelette. Olly was the only twenty-first century teenager who knew Semaphore and a bit of Esperanto.

Until James, Olly's best friend had been a pensioner.

When James opened his bedroom window he couldn't hear a Latin American band or steel drums. The road was always quiet. It was one of the things people paid for. No drunks on benches, no take away packaging or kebab smell trailing into dawn, and no noise except ride-on lawnmowers.

London without the edge.

Not exciting enough for Faith. He hoped she wasn't getting more excitement than she wanted. Sometimes she forgot how she looked to the world: small, young and innocent in spite of the carefully styled, blonde spikes – which were bendy when you tested them.

The thoughts reminded him of Eleanor, Olly and the argument. And one moment the night before. But it didn't last long. At the question about summer holidays – which felt like a desperate way to end a silence – Eleanor prodded the tablecloth with her fork.

"My parents are splitting up," she said. "So I'll get two."

It was hard to know how to react, especially with her face lowered to examine the prick marks in the red fabric. James settled for a non-verbal sound through the nose and hoped it was encouraging and supportive.

She smoothed fair hair behind her ear even though it lay perfectly shaped and under control.

"Two Christmases. Two birthdays." She sipped her iced water. "Two mothers."

James still found all that hard to imagine every time.

"That's tough," he said, and wished he could do better than American TV.

"No," she said, shaking her head and furrowing her forehead. "It isn't. I am."

"O.K.," he said, vaguely, and nodded. Mentally deleting every possible follow-up from *That's all right then* to *No kidding.*

"You'll find out," she said. "You have to be. You've had it easy."

Which he thought was presumptuous, and a bit patronising. But generally true, apart from the death in Sweden and the redundancy. And Physics. She didn't ask anything about his life because she seemed to think she knew – that there wasn't much to know.

At that point the waiter came over to ask if everything was all right with the meal.

"Great, thanks," James said.

Silence. It settled over their table like their own

personal rain cloud, while the others basked in sun. Eleanor gathered a small forkful of salad leaves. James knew she wouldn't want him feeling sorry for her, asking for more detail or recommending his mother's services – even though it would take an expert to help Eleanor Langridge, or persuade her she needed help of any kind.

He almost asked her a different question because he really wanted to know. Could she shed light on a mystery as deep as the Kennedy assassinations? Why had she agreed to go out with him? Could it be because according to Faith, her friends thought he was *"quite fit really for a loser"* and had *"nice hair if you'd just comb it"*? Faith also thought he was funny but he couldn't imagine how to make Eleanor laugh.

James couldn't concentrate on his revision guide. He pressed the remote on his TV to hear the crowd on the Mall waiting for the kiss on the balcony. James tried to imagine kissing Eleanor. He could have gone for the parting peck, the sexless goodnight, couldn't he? She wouldn't actually have slapped him. (Or would she?) But by then he'd taken so many verbal and silent slaps that it would have felt like kissing the headmistress at the end of a disciplinary.

He looked at his phone, flat and black on the bed where he'd dropped it. No Faith.

"Call," he told her. "Just call!" He put the message in a text but the phone lay flat and black as ever. Stephen and Agnetha were the dictionary definition of reasonable. Flexible. Fair. So why did Faith have to behave as if pushing boundaries was an Olympic event and there was a qualifying standard to meet?

Not so long ago she'd jump up like a puppy when he walked into the room.

James turned off the TV, lay back and closed his eyes, but Faith was still there – jumping, but no one in the crowd seemed to see.

His phone sounded suddenly. Olly.

"Hey," said James, and wondered what came next, other than *"Is he dead then?"*

"Hey."

Olly seemed unusually short of words.

"Where are you?"

"Outside the hospital. Waiting."

James thought Olly sounded as if he was in New Zealand and there was way too much space between them.

"Sorry."

"Yeah."

"You were… close."

"Yeah. Are. Can you stay close to dead people?" asked Olly. "Or get closer once they're dead?"

"Agnetha is. To her sister. I think."

"Ah," said Olly, and James heard him remembering. Other people's tragedies were so small outside the epicentre. James wanted to feel more for Olly too. Find a few words.

"I want to," said Olly.

"Yeah," said James.

"How's the party?"

"Dunno. I'm doing Chemistry."

"WHAT!" Suddenly Olly might have been in the doorway. "Boff."

"Yeah, right."

James didn't mention the matter of Eleanor Langridge. Olly sounded more like himself again – more than usual, in a way.

"Might not make it," said Olly. "The party."

"No," said James. "Sorry about Heinz."

"Yeah," said Olly. "Not full of beans any more."

James smiled as he put down the phone. Agnetha would say Olly needed to talk about his feelings but he supposed you could only do that if you'd found some words that labelled them. Even Agnetha said therapy had too many labels.

James decided to read Shakespeare instead. It was starting to make a strange kind of sense and when it did, it packed a punch and had more to say than Olly about the big things. Lying on the bed with Othello, James glanced outside and saw the grey sky still hadn't turned to rain. Maybe he'd wander over to the barbecue soon, and send his dad back on house phone duty. If he inhaled deeply enough, he thought he could almost smell the hot charcoal on the air, and the fat sizzling. Brains needed fuel after all.

SIX

Hema would have liked to walk briskly, the way her father would tell her to. He'd be far from happy about her being out alone at all. She hoped one of her parents would understand that she had the right to free herself from Anant. To make her own choices and find her own way.

She clamped her shoulder bag down to her hips with one arm.

"Got your umbrella?" Louis would ask, if he knew.

Not for rain, because in Mauritius, he told her, *"the rain was more sudden than a quarrel"* and cleared up much more quickly. Clothes soon dried in sun. In London, an umbrella was supposed to be a weapon, and the idea was that if she carried it, wielded it as if she was ready to use it, maniacs would give her a swerve and pick on someone else.

Obediently, Hema took her umbrella from her bag, rolled up – like an old policeman's truncheon apart from the big, bright spots. She didn't suppose she looked very menacing. If she'd been looking round warily since she left Hyde Park, it was for Anant rather than muggers (who might be in a better mood than usual today, and taking a day off from mugging). She thought of the people working, in near-empty shopping centres or garages. Maybe they were treating the day like Christmas Eve and having long breaks – not for mince pies and sherry but TV catch-ups.

Now that she was out of the park (and it had taken some persistence to dodge and beg her way out) and heading for Buckingham Palace, Hema felt a sense of relief and adventure. She might not get much of a view but when the couple left for Clarence House she might catch a glimpse of flesh and fabric, paint and gold that wasn't just magnified on TV. Something to tell her children about one day.

"They moved the barriers," said a woman, walking alongside.

A little breathless, lumbering but determined, she seemed to be with a friend or sister, who added optimistically, "Some people probably went home after the fly past."

"Fly past?" Hema echoed, puzzled.

"Old R.A.F. Spitfires and Wellingtons from the Battle of Britain," was the answer.

"And new ones too!"

"War planes?" asked Hema, but they'd been separated now by others on the move. Hema walked on. It seemed bizarre to celebrate love and the start of a couple's new life together, with bombers and fighter planes that brought death. She was glad she'd missed them.

So the half million were closer now, gathered at the foot of the balcony and trailing back in a circle that spilt out behind. But Hema was still at the tail end. And as she positioned herself where she could, with no chance of leaning or tiptoeing her way to a view, she started to feel stupid after all.

Just enjoy it, she told herself. *This is atmosphere*. It was a loud crowd, not shouting but chatting, eating as they stood, laughing and exchanging conversation with strangers. Just as they were in the park, but this felt different because these were the seriously committed. The planners, campers, early risers. Somewhere ahead of her were people who'd seen the kiss, the lace on the dress, and the fibres on the bearskins of the Coldstream Guards. People close enough to call and be heard on the balcony.

"Eighty percent of people in the U.K. support the monarchy," Celeste had read or heard that morning.

"Yes, but why?" Hema had asked.

"It's a tradition," Louis answered. "Pomp and circumstance. It's what tourists come here for."

"They come for The Tower of London," said Hema, "and the history. It wouldn't matter if the Queen wasn't actually here. People could pay to look round her bedroom, and see where she used to sleep. That'd be a lot more interesting than a flag on top of the palace."

"You'd like to turn the palace into a theme park, I suppose?" cried Celeste.

Louis wasn't happy either. "What are they teaching you at school?"

"Nothing," said Hema, which wasn't what her parents wanted to hear. "I mean, I'm thinking for myself."

"People in this country don't know how lucky they are," Louis complained.

"Yes, but we don't have to swap a Queen for a dictator like Gadaffi," said Hema. "Couldn't we be like France and just have a government?"

Her parents didn't like France because Sarkozy was what her dad called *"a playboy"*. And Muslims couldn't wear the burkah there, which Hema agreed was a disgrace.

"There are more French atheists," said Celeste. "And more cigarette smokers!"

"Even if there are," said Hema, trying not to smile, "it doesn't necessarily follow. If we became a republic, people wouldn't suddenly lose their faith and take up smoking."

"Ha!" laughed Louis. "Too smart for her own good!" But he said it proudly.

"If you're going to spring political debates on us," said Celeste, "give me notice and I'll read up."

Celeste was an Internet junkie these days and couldn't be persuaded that it wasn't always a hundred percent reliable.

The discussion had got lost in preparations – for their day in front of the TV and hers in town with Anant.

"Bring him back for supper later," called Celeste.

Thinking about that made Hema hungry. She tried to manage her mother's packed lunch while she waited for the newly-weds to reappear. There was far too much for one, and remembering Anant's opinion made everything seem oilier than usual. She was wiping her greasy fingers and mouth when she looked up at the sound of a helicopter overhead. A man behind her was pointing upwards and she heard him say, "RAF, Search and Rescue."

Of course – Prince William's job. A big improvement, thought Hema, on the bombers. Suddenly she heard and felt a Mexican wave of sound and movement that meant excitement. Arousal. Some kind of action. Someone was heading her way and it couldn't just be Edward and Sophie.

She heard about the sports car and the number plate joke, JU5T WED, long before there was anything to see. And the man behind was telling people "Aston Martin!" so he must have X-ray vision, inside information or an image on a phone screen. Hema felt a stirring of curiosity and elation – and fear that whatever was coming, she wouldn't see it, and wouldn't know it had gone until shoulders fell.

From the behaviour of the crowd she could tell where the car must be, but still she saw nothing. Hema knew this was her last chance to salvage something from the day. She did all she could, fish-like, not pushing but easing through. Not so much advancing as finding an angle that opened up a chink. And as Kate and William went past in their open-topped sports car, she saw... enough. Enough to tell, from the backs of two heads, that it was them. Enough to tell they were relaxed and happy and it was real after all.

She laughed at herself. She was getting as bad as her mother! It was the hysteria, cheerful and good-humoured as it was, infecting her. They were nothing to her. How could they be? How were their lives in any way connected with hers?

But still she could not shake the pleasure away. She had made it pay off. Not so stupid after all.

"No photo!" her mother would cry. As if she should have barged into the front row and got a full frontal shot of the whites of their teeth.

People around her were smiling, and talking about the number plate which Hema hadn't even glimpsed. She realised that everyone was with someone – a husband, a sister, a friend, a mother or daughter. It wasn't a place to be alone.

She didn't care now how many other Royals might emerge as part of the supporting cast. She'd seen the big stars. Zipping up her bag, Hema moved away towards the tube. Time to go home and explain herself.

Faith fancied a take away coffee but Costa and Starbucks were queued up like January sales. As she headed for the tube station she realised she'd need a new phone and urgently, irresistibly. James was good when it came to deals, although he was hopeless with his own phone and didn't even know where it was half the time.

People clogged the entrance behind the barriers and progress was slow. Faith felt in her back pocket for her ticket. Nothing there either side. Of course not. Toilet floor, remember! She didn't risk that any more. Stepping back out of the crowd, she went through her purse. Two pounds twenty-four and a hair grip. The zip-up pocket where she'd started to keep important things was open and empty. So where had she put her ticket?

No hole in the lining of her bag. Nothing caught round in an old tissue. Start again, she told herself, but she was panicking now because it wasn't there. Breathing out but still feeling a fluttery tightness in her chest, Faith found a memory from a few hours earlier. Like a crime victim watching a TV re-enactment, she saw herself, with Ayesha and Tash. Heard the laughter, as they exited the station, about a supply teacher who according to Ayesha, couldn't spell and looked like a hippy. Tash did an impression, hand in the air: *"Maidens, desist!"* She'd felt the hint of a blush that kept her eyes down because she'd liked him. And with the remembered blush she felt it again – her fingers fitting the ticket into a back pocket.

Just like her phone.

A thief in the crowd! A hand that wasn't hers had slipped in too.

"I was robbed," she said, to no one in particular. And the words came back: *So out of order! Outrageous!*

Everyone had gone through the barrier now except a girl: older than her, exotic-looking with glossy waves of black hair and wide brown eyes.

"Are you all right?" she asked.

Annoyingly, a sob broke out and Faith didn't quite scoop it back.

"I've got no ticket. My phone's gone too. And I've got no money – almost no money."

"Are you sure?"

For a moment Faith thought she was going to be told to check again. She felt like a child who couldn't find her goggles in the changing room when they were on her head. She half-expected the girl to leave her searching and go on through the barrier, but she didn't. She waited.

"No good?" she asked.

Faith only risked a shake of the head.

"Where do you live?" asked the girl. "How much money do you need for a ticket? Will a fiver do?"

Faith was staring. Was she mad?

"Five pounds?" repeated the girl, as if she mistook her for someone Polish, Bulgarian... "For a new ticket?"

Faith thought this girl might be almost a woman but she had no idea what being streetwise meant! She must be new to London herself. Now she was holding out a five pound note.

"I'm English," said Faith.

"Oh." Now the girl looked puzzled.

"I just couldn't believe my ears, you know? You, offering me money like that, with all the scammers around. Nobody does that. Trusts people, I mean."

The girl shrugged lightly. "So I'm a mug. If you're a scammer."

Faith saw her look around as if there might be more like her lurking. But she didn't withdraw the five pound note folded in her hand.

"No!" cried Faith. "I'm really not. It's just that my dad has told me never to fall for that kind of thing." She took the money. "I think they must both have been in the same back pocket, my ticket and my phone," she said. "Thanks so much, really!"

"No problem."

"Give me your address and I'll pay you back."

"Don't worry. There's no need."

Faith realised the scammers made the same offer. "I really will pay you back. My family's got money. Dad'll want to thank you."

"Really," said the girl. "Forget it."

Faith thought how striking she was. And nice, and trusting. And crazy.

"Which way are you going?"

It turned out they were travelling in the same direction. As they moved along the tunnel past the film posters, they talked royal kisses and Aston Martins.

When they reached the platform the board said eight minutes and there was nowhere to sit. Not too many places to stand either. Faith found herself up close and personal with the girl who'd paid for the ticket now sealed inside her bag.

"I'm Hema," said the girl.

"Thanks, Hema. It's really kind of you. I'm Faith." Wondering whether Hema might be Muslim, Faith became unusually sheepish. "Embarrassing name," she added. "Mine, I mean."

"It's beautiful," said Hema, and Faith thought she meant it.

"Shaz Parminter-Adams told me I might as well be called Religion." Faith realised she sounded pathetic and tried to grin. "I said, *"You wait till Michelle Obama visits!"* That wiped her smile 'cos she didn't get it."

"I do," said Hema. "And faith is a big, wide word – full of light, not rules."

Faith smiled, wondering whether that would sound as serious and deep if she said it, herself, to Shaz and her mates. She could imagine them laughing all the way down the corridor. It was dignity that made the difference and maybe she could cultivate it but she didn't know how.

"Thanks," she said.

Hema repeated the faith sentence in her head, like a line from a film that had registered and she wanted to remember. Why couldn't she think like that, talk like that, when Anant was around? Probably because he'd twist his face into the kind of incomprehension that was a slur. A jeer.

"This Shaz Parminter-Adams and her crowd," Hema told the small, blonde girl, "you want to jettison them. Get shot of them, my dad would say."

The three years between them made her stronger and calmer than she expected to feel.

"I know," said the girl. "Thanks."

"You're bigger than they are."

They both smiled, given Faith's height, or lack of it, accentuated by a basketball type looming over her and chewing like a cow.

Once the train finally pulled in, they managed to stay together, standing but straight, without jostling, bad breath or baggage attack. Hema felt an obligation. She wasn't going to abandon a thirteen-year-old who'd been robbed, especially as they lived a few miles apart. She thought Faith's parents must be liberal: free and easy, with money and all kinds of freedoms. The kind who gave kids space and let them explore it all, dark corners included.

And this Faith was a child, really – but full of the confidence moneyed kids grew up with, especially if they'd fit on the cover of *Sugar* magazine. A child who thought she was more streetwise than Hema because she could do anything and be anything she wanted.

Hema hadn't said so to Faith, but her parents wouldn't have allowed her out like that at thirteen. They wouldn't be happy now if they knew she was alone – or rather, the stand-in adult with no protector of her own.

Celeste had replied to her reassuring text with a message full of bubbles. *Great day*, it said. Well, good. They deserved one. Hema smiled to think of them wedged together on the sofa, revellers too.

On the tube people were loud and gregarious. It wasn't just that travel today was a communal experience, thought Hema. So was the day itself . Faith was chatty too, curious, admiring.

"I like your sandals."

Soon afterwards: "Nice ring."

Hema recognised a white girl's fascination with her otherness. She'd already explained about Mauritius, her voice low because she wasn't the kind to perform to an audience the way others were doing. Now, as they stood in the carriage, holding on, it was getting more personal.

"Have you got a boyfriend?" asked Faith.

Hema wouldn't ask a stranger that but this girl was young and different. More open than she'd ever been.

"Wouldn't I be with him, if I had?" she evaded. Then she smiled, so that the girl wouldn't feel snubbed. "I came up with him but we had a... fall-out. I ended the relationship."

She could see Faith was excited. It made Hema feel bolder, and glad.

"Why?" tried Faith, after a few moments of looking around the carriage and then back to Hema.

"Reasons," Hema told her, playing with the amber ring she'd admired. "Sometimes you need a... catalyst. Something to bring things together – or to a conclusion."

"Like a wedding?"

"I guess it could go either way."

They agreed that there must have been plenty of proposals today already.

"Maybe more to come," said a woman who apologised and said she couldn't help overhearing. "It's early yet."

"You're hopeful!" laughed her friend.

"You got a street party to go to, girls?" asked the optimist.

Hema shook her head. Not that she knew of. And her parents wouldn't want her going alone, even if there was, in case there were youths with hoodies and cans.

"I have," said Faith, "a posh one." Hema saw her smile with the kind of brightness she hadn't seen before. "Why don't you come? Dad'll drive you back if he's sober. Or get you a taxi. They owe you..."

"I don't think I should," said Hema. "Thank you anyway."

"Why not?" Faith asked her, genuinely wondering, and she couldn't answer. Her father couldn't fret about the neighbourhood. She could see what it was like, and then make an exit, be home long before dark.

"Yes, why not?" she said. "Thank you. If you're sure."

At the street party the weather hadn't improved much, but James thought the laughter was ringing a lot less false. Conversation had become more fluid. Agnetha seemed to be enjoying the fruit punch, the lemon and orange segments bobbing against her lipstick as she drank.

"No one admits to concocting it but it's a lot stronger than Pimm's," she warned James. "Hold on to your legs."

A man in a soft cardigan butted in with the usual openers about how lovely it was to see them. Agnetha introduced him to James – but James's name was the only one of the two she got right. Not Bob but Brian! As the poor guy turned away to the drinks table, James wagged a finger at his mother.

James was reminded of Eleanor. And all the mistakes she wouldn't allow past her the night before.

"*George VI, not V,*" she'd corrected while spearing tomato. Eleanor's godfather was a relative of someone on the production team that made the Oscar-winning film.

"*I don't agree,*" she'd interrupted, because he'd said single-sex schools were unhealthy and weird. "*Boys hold girls back. They dominate and distract. It's what every study shows.*"

"*Of course it is!*" she'd said, when he'd queried fashion as an art form. "*Have you ever looked at a cat walk collection?*"

Apparently Eleanor knew more about everything than most cabinet ministers ever learned about their own department.

James was busy reliving put-downs when he saw Stephen approaching, hurrying towards them in his chinos and two-tone gangster shoes, smiling and waving a phone like a flag.

"I don't think Faith's been abducted for white slave trafficking after all," James told Agnetha.

Smiling with relief, he watched his mother almost run to his father, as fast as heels allowed.

"She's fine," Stephen told them. "It's been a bad day but she's been rescued."

"By Horse Guards?" he asked.

"By someone called Hema. I've told Faith to bring her back here to the party so I can pay her back."

"Sounds like a story," said James, imagining how melodramatic his sister would make it. He couldn't picture someone called Hema because he'd never heard the name before. Stephen explained to Daph and Joel that Faith had fallen out with her friends and had her phone stolen along with her train ticket. And seen nothing.

"She'll have to try again when Charles is crowned," said Daph.

"Will anyone bother about that?" asked James, which seemed to deepen the colour of Joel's cheeks. "Anyway, might he abdicate and hand over to William?"

"Ridiculous nonsense dreamed up by the media!" scoffed Joel. "Unconstitutional. Why should he? Just because William's the tabloids' darling? That'd change soon enough."

James nodded at a good point, but Joel was warming to his subject, his cheeks almost florid. Agnetha tried to change the subject by suggesting that no state occasion would ever match Diana's funeral.

Whoosh! Match to petrol!

"Should never have married him!" cried Joel. "Far too unstable. Did an enormous amount of damage."

James looked at his mother, hoping the punch didn't bring tears back to the surface.

"But she was the most glamorous Royal ever," Stephen said, arm round Agnetha. "She must have doubled the value of the brand.

"She wasn't a Royal!" objected Daph. "That was the point!"

Meanwhile Joel was echoing, "Brand! Some things can't be reduced to marketing, you know!"

That was when a slick yellow car slid up at entourage pace. Conversation tailed away. People turned. Looked. James cast around the faces for clues. Who? What?

The car pulled up at the edge of the party area. It was an old Lotus Elan, Seventies style, low-slung and intimate. James wouldn't have been surprised to see a Chelsea player at the wheel with a WAG. But it was the driver who was female, in shades.

James thought he heard his father swear very quietly. Still everyone waited. Only the music played on.

Then for the first time James saw the passenger, and recognised him – a dog walker he hadn't seen for a while, a banker, city type. He lived at the house nearest to the parked vehicle: the giant white, six or seven bedroom mansion set back along a rhododendron drive.

This wasn't his car. Didn't he drive a roller? What was going on?

"He hasn't still got a remote for the gates?" Stephen whispered to Agnetha.

"Poor Louisa," murmured Agnetha.

"What?" asked James.

"Louisa's his wife," muttered Stephen behind his hand.

"Ah," said James. He was getting a picture: a middle-aged woman, waxed body warmer, flat grey hair. Now that he thought about it, she'd been the one walking the

Great Dane recently. So the driver of the Lotus Elan wasn't a WAG. This was TOW. The Other Woman.

Joel was muttering the name of Katie Price but the woman who slid out of the driver's seat was older and less plastic. Her hair was as black as her dress and she might be Italian.

"No one invited him, did they?" asked Agnetha.

Stephen looked helpless.

"I'm going to see Louisa," said Agnetha purposefully, "if she'll let me in."

James thought, as she crossed the road, that their neighbours might think twice about opening their mouths to a therapist. In conversation with Agnetha he often stuck to You Tube: guys in underpants making angel wings in snow, babies laughing and cats seeing off crocodiles. Obviously there were things his parents didn't tell him either.

Great Dane man had left his wife for an Italian who looked, now that she removed her sunglasses, as if she might bite the nearest neck. And had turned up at the street party to shake it up. Pretty successfully.

"Not very tactful, mate," said Stephen, as Great Dane man unfolded himself from the car and took the vampire's hand.

"The thing is, Patrick, we're celebrating, you know?" said Joel, clearing his throat and speaking at the back of it. "Bonhomie and neighbourly... that's the idea."

"Come on, guys," said Patrick. "We're entitled."

Patrick smiled. His hair was white and floppy and James thought he smelt more powerfully fragrant than his new woman. His clothes were brand new. James supposed he must be nearly sixty.

"That's still my house too."

"That's as maybe, Patrick..." began Joel.

"But what about Louisa?" finished Daph.

"She said she wasn't coming."

James guessed that was a shortened and edited version.

"Ah," said Joel. "I see."

"This is Lucia," said Patrick.

He tried to toss his hair back without a free hand to assist, which made him look less like a beauty on a shampoo ad than a horse. Then he pulled three bottles out from a gift bag with tasselled handles, one after another, and placed them on the trestle table.

Interesting, thought James. Even he knew the name on the bottles meant big money and bigger reputation. Could they buy their way in?

"Anyone like some of this?" asked Patrick, and the geniality was coming more naturally now. He seemed to be gaining confidence.

A couple of people certainly did. The cork-popping was professional standard and he knew how to pour it too. Lucia got the first glass but the next few to be filled were all taken. James realised his father didn't know what to do for a moment, but when Lucia offered him a glass with a smile, he took it.

James gave him a look.

"Played much golf lately?" asked one of the other men, and that was it. Patrick was re-integrated. Absorbed. Back in the fold. They were star guests, in fact. And if the other women hated Lucia for her figure, hair, tan, dress or husband-stealing they weren't showing it. Not a soap episode after all. Manners or sham, the important thing was smoothing over. And there were dresses in cathedrals to talk about.

James found himself doing what could best be described as mooching, around the tables with their paper cloths fidgeting at the tips. He picked at the finger food, keeping his head down so that no one read eye contact as encouragement to ask about exams or career plans. He was running out of variations on *"Not sure,"* other than the more precise, *"I don't know."*

But all at once the street party seemed to be livening up quite dramatically, with the volume right up on *La Vida Loca*.

Daph and Joel started to respond with some interesting moves, which in her case began at the hips but stretched up to fingers casting spells. Joel's were boxer style, both fists pushing weights chest-high as he sang along with the chorus. Below his overhanging stomach, his feet angled like bricks on hinges, parallel one minute and penguin-splayed the next. If Faith had been there, James would be avoiding eye contact in case his mouth couldn't hold in the laughter.

Olly would say, *"Bizarre."* James imagined telling him what he'd missed and Olly's big mouth doing its hippo thing. He knew he'd be hurting. But which was worse – bereavement or betrayal? Sometimes he thought there was so much to look forward to, but as Agnetha said, *"Only a child expects blue sky and roses all year round."*

She hadn't come back yet so she must be comforting Louisa. Or waiting to be admitted through the security gates – unless she was climbing them. Squash and Pilates kept her fit enough.

Stephen was dancing now, with the woman who apparently dreamed up the whole idea of the party. The word *excruciating* sprang to mind.

"Come on, James!" called Joel. "Teach us some hip hop. Don't you have to blag?"

"Swag," said James. "But don't ask me how."

"Poor James," said Daph. "He's surrounded by old fogeys."

"Lucia! Lucia's his generation, more or less!" cried Joel.

Which was not very tactful, given how close she was behind him. Or more importantly, how likely it was that Patrick, attentive at her shoulder, would hear.

Lucia turned. James looked away. But she was moving towards him, hands free, and Patrick was holding two glasses and watching.

The word *Help* went through James's head. And the protest, *"I'm not a fan of Twilight."*

Then he heard his name, louder than the music.

"Hey!" he cried. "Sprite!"

His sister looked young and small, but not traumatised. And beside her – just a step behind now as Faith started to scamper – was her guardian angel.

SEVEN

Olly knew where to find the coin because he kept things that mattered in an old biscuit tin that once held red and yellow building bricks. There wasn't much.

A birthday card from his gran, Heinz's bride, and Heinz too.

His Cub badges, because he didn't have as many as some boys but there were some no one else earned, like Flower Arranger, because Heinz taught him that, and Entertainer because of the magic tricks and jokes.

A drawing, folded up, of an apple and an orange, because it was the only picture he'd done in primary school that made it onto a display board.

The autograph of an international scrum half, like a section of the line on a life-support machine.

And the three penny bit. Nothing special about it. Small and ochre, with edges that might have been chewed. A very young Queen on the back. Heinz used to call him Thruppence when he was small. He'd never said why and it was too late to ask but Olly liked it and on his third birthday Heinz gave him the coin.

"I've been keeping it," he said, "until you were too big to eat it."

Small Olly went to A and E three times when objects disappeared down his throat and Heinz always blamed himself.

Now Olly polished the coin with spit, and a tissue that broke up. But he liked the rusty ordinariness of it. No need for gleaming. His father's drill was in the shed. Olly went outside, heard the party hotting up, selected the finest drill blade and screwed it in. Pulling out a twenty pence piece from his pocket, he practised on that. Fouled up. Got the measure of the task. Went indoors for Blu-tack to fix it down so he didn't have to hold it and avoid his finger. Tried again, without allowing himself to think about failure, because it was the only three penny bit he had and if he messed it up he'd hate himself. Straight through, clear and round. He could set himself up as an ear piercer for girls, competitive rates. Olly pictured Eleanor Langridge's ears, the prettiest he knew, small and soft. As if!

Leaving the drill lying in the midst of the mess that was his father's shed, Olly went back indoors. Ribbon would do. A chain would be better. In his mother's jewellery box he found a cross she never wore, with a darkened chain. Olly knew he could ask but he didn't want to use the words, hear them out loud. His three penny bit, his granddad, his memories. She wouldn't mind. She wouldn't even notice. He slipped the chain free and threaded it. Just right. He fastened it round his neck, and tucked it down underneath the T-shirt. Not cold exactly, but firm.

"Thanks, Heinz," he said.

He put a post-it note in the box: *Borrowed a spare chain.* And added a smiley.

Olly remembered the surprisingly funky music from the street party and supposed he might go along later. Wakes were parties for the dead, and Heinz would like people dancing. Olly tried sending James a text but his phone was off – or drowned out by the nightclub beat. He might need rescuing, thought Olly, from the Brigadier's wife. And his moves might be worth capturing on camera.

It crossed his mind that Eleanor might not quite be a resident, buts she was certainly a local. No one would object to him bringing her along as a (suitably classy) guest. Except, of course, Eleanor.

And possibly James. He didn't want to replay that scene because it felt cut in from a different film. The two of them didn't do that. And he didn't want to do it again.

Faint heart never won fair lady. It was Heinz in his head. For a German he'd been full of English phrases that might be medieval.

"Good point, Heinz," said Olly, touching the bronze round his neck. He'd better wash his hair.

James knew Faith was watching him looking at Hema, and smiling. Could she tell? Could everyone? It must be obvious, transparent. He felt like Prince William at the altar except that there'd been no Harry to tip him off, warn him. No preparation. And no white dress but she was an angel anyway.

James had no idea where the name came from but Hema made him think of five star holidays in sunshine. Palm trees, spiked grass, coconuts and melons. Thick, warm sweetness on his tongue. Her eyes were wide and brown, her eyelashes so long and black she could package them in a kit, for airheads like Sprite to buy. But she looked beside him, beyond, down and around. She was shy; he could see that. But Faith was doing enough talking for three.

And all he'd said was, "Hullo."

Stephen thanked her.

"No problem, honestly. I was there..."

Her voice was deeper than he'd expected, but quiet.

James almost had to strain to hear it against the drum and bass.

"Let me pay you back the cost of the train fare." Stephen pulled out his wallet.

"Really, there's no need."

Faith obviously thought there was and told their father how much he owed.

"I said you'd give her a lift home later too," said Faith. "Or get her a taxi if you're off your face." She grinned. "Which you might be already, judging by your dancing."

"Less of your cheek!" said Stephen, and gave Hema a ten pound note, a crisp one. "Please take it. And of course, we'll see that you get home safely. Where is...?"

"Can I get a new phone tomorrow, Dad?" asked Faith.

James could see she was enjoying herself now.

"We'll see," Stephen said. "A cheap one. Basic. You know, brick-style, like Mum's."

Stephen winked at Hema. James was almost shocked, but Faith objected first, with an elbow that nearly spilt his drink.

"Behave!" she told him.

"Can I get you a drink, Hema?" Stephen asked.

Come on, James told himself. Such an obvious question and he should have asked her first. He reminded himself to remember the everyday things. But he supposed his father had taken decades to develop this assurance. James had never seen him quite so smooth; Hema must think he was charming.

Was that what Lucia thought of Patrick?

Stephen was running through the options, recommending the top of the range champagne while there was still some left, although privately James thought it tasted like pear drops without the sugar.

"I'll have some," said Faith. Stephen pretended not to hear.

"I don't drink alcohol," said Hema. "Fruit juice would be fine."

"Why?" asked Faith.

James gave her a look but she seemed too awestruck to be accusing.

"Mind your own business, Sprite," he told her.

He was nearer than his father to the orange juice and started to pour a glass. He smiled. A break at last! And he didn't spill any.

She thanked him. It was crowded around the table so he edged away and she followed, leaving Stephen and Faith to negotiations.

"Dad, I'm a teenager!"

"Five whole years too young for alcohol."

"Dad, do you still not know what day it is?!"

As they found a little space, the music changed to something less strident and less likely to rattle glasses.

"My sister isn't really a brat," James told her, because he guessed she didn't talk to her father like that. "She's soft underneath. She wants to be a vet."

"Yes," said Hema. "She told me."

James wished he knew what else they'd shared. More on Faith's side than hers, he imagined. He didn't want to probe, or ask the standard questions he'd been dodging himself. So he just looked encouraging for a moment. She looked around her and he wished he knew what she made of it all. *Loaded? Upper class? Clueless?* Could she see beyond?

"Did you have a good view?" he asked. "Of the wedding?"

"No," she said, and he thought there might have been more, but Faith called over, a small glass of champagne in her hand. Her smile was triumphant.

"Hema dumped her boyfriend in Hyde Park!" she informed him.

"Faith," he muttered, reproachful.

Was Hema embarrassed? He wouldn't blame her but she only smiled, and didn't deny.

"Never tell my sister any secrets," said James. "I learned that when I was eight."

"I don't tell anyone my secrets," said Hema, and cast her eyes down on the juice.

James believed her. But what were her secrets? Not dark, he thought, but the opposite – whatever that was. Airy and scented. In his head he heard Olly: *"Get a grip!"*

Hema sipped her juice but he could see she wasn't thirsty.

"Have you got GCSEs?" he asked her, and she nodded, so they got it over with: the inevitable, the faces pulled.

Only the basics overlapped. She was doing Art, Italian and Textiles. Of course she was! He would have asked her to say something in Italian but he might sound like a seven-year-old.

Hema listened carefully, looking for clues, but she couldn't tell much from his subjects – when he finally recalled the last one on the list.

"Oh, and P.E," he remembered. "I'm not an ace at anything. I can run a bit but Dad's got more stamina."

She noticed that he didn't seem to expect twelve A stars. Or even have favourites.

"I haven't found it yet," he said, as if he read her thoughts. "You know, that thing that does it for you. The passion that drives you on to something. My mum says I will. I think my dad despairs."

Hema smiled. His father didn't seem the despairing type, dancing with Faith in a way designed to make her groan.

"I don't know yet, what I'll be," she said, "but I have a kind of passion for learning. Discovering – people, places, art and history. And ideas, so many ideas."

She'd never talked to Anant like this! She'd never talked like this at all!

He gave her a look that made her glad. What was it, Hema wondered – understanding? He nodded as if he meant it.

"It's exciting when you put it like that."

"Yes. It is."

Hema wouldn't have known this boy was related to Sprite. The nickname suited Faith for now, but she could be beautiful soon. And she could imagine Celeste and Shireen's giggles and facials over their father, who would certainly be labelled *"a dish"*. She didn't think James would qualify, unless he turned out to be a prince. But she liked his face.

He was so much scruffier than anyone else at the street party that if he'd been a couple of years older she might have thought he'd come to fix something. Her dad, who had a hundred names for colours to identify the garments on the rail, would call his hair chestnut, but it needed attention. His blue-grey eyes locked on as if they took everything in. Including her.

Faith had made it obvious that she loved her big brother and Hema could see why anyone would. She thought the soft one of the two was probably him. Suddenly she imagined her mother verging on hysteria. A private road, a detached house hidden by trees and an independent school with a clock tower and observatory. And a boy called James with a newsreader's accent.

A nice boy, then! But his eyes said she'd be right.

"I'm guessing you've been tipped off about me," he told her, and gave his sister a warning smile. "But you know what they say about sources. They're not always reliable."

"No," Hema said, wishing she was quicker, sharper.

She could have said something about trying to think critically and make her own judgement but it was too full-on. They'd only just met and she didn't want him to think he was being evaluated. Even if that meant five stars. But she couldn't just keep smiling wordlessly through conversation openings – unless she wanted to bring them all to a close. And look empty. Was she looking admiring?

"Talking of sauces," he told her, "the chilli stuff is good." One finger checked for traces round his mouth. "Mum made the cashew burgers. We're all vegetarian – whole family, except my brother, who's converted to kebabs now he's at uni."

"I ate an enormous lunch," she said. "My mum packed it for two."

"I expect Faith already asked you why you dumped him," said James. Direct. She didn't mind.

"Yes, but I didn't tell her much."

"That must have frustrated her." He grinned at the sister in question, who was giving him a very awkward and attention-grabbing wink from a few paces away. "We're being watched," he said. "Sorry."

Hema didn't care. It crossed her mind that Faith had set them up, not from the start of course, but on the tube. She gave her a smile. But she told herself he was simply polite, well brought up. She lowered her eyes because they might be giving away too much, more than he wanted.

"I didn't want to be dominated," she told the ground, and looked up, wondering whether he'd heard, or was following. "That was the problem with Anant. Respect shouldn't be an issue, should it? More of a minimum requirement."

"Basic," he said, "all round, global, across all boundaries."

She smiled so widely it felt reckless.

There was no answer at Eleanor's place but from an upstairs window Olly could hear some familiar classical music, the kind that made a soundtrack for movie funerals and break-ups. Someone was making a point for someone else's benefit.

He stood below the doorstep, which was coffin-deep and worn. Savage-looking plants that might have escaped from desert landscapes stood guard, one on each side of him. The wall was dressed with camellias, and petals scattered the gravel, browning. It was one of those old, three storey houses that extended back and back, and could hide whole families in annexes behind bookcases. In fact Eleanor's parents could have half each and just kick on a dividing wall now and then.

Olly felt oddly new. His hair was so clean he could smell it even with the barbecue tang on the air. Orange blossom couldn't compete! He left jasmine standing!

But would Eleanor leave him standing, and pretend she hadn't heard the gravel or the doorbell? He was surprised she didn't stick her nose out of the window, wondering what could possibly smell so good. He'd joked with James once, about her treading in a lot of dog shit because her nose was so high in the air she wouldn't smell it. Eleanor was stuck-up. And brittle, prickly and scathing. And whatever she said, James wasn't thick and insensitive. He could see that for James an hour with Eleanor would be like falling through a window and coming out with shards of glass jabbing in all over.

But no one was perfect. Olly's mum said her parents were at war and he knew how to survive all that. Olly thought he might have inherited a sense of humour from Heinz. Admittedly the evidence suggested that Eleanor's wasn't very well developed, but maybe he could give her something to laugh about.

Looking at the door, he pictured her. Elegant, yes, but an elongated pixie, with that little, pointed nose and great big eyes that could shrivel a Dalek.

He braced himself as the door opened. Force field in place. But Eleanor looked different. Hard as it was to imagine, he thought she might have been crying. She wasn't wearing make-up, apart from the sheen on her lips. Had she applied that a moment ago, for him?

"Yes?" she said, as if he'd better not be a Jehovah's Witness.

"I didn't interrupt your revision, did I?"

"Since I have eleven papers in May," she said, "yes."

"You didn't see the wedding then?"

"It didn't seem the best investment of time." She smoothed her hair back from her head like a swimmer. "Can't anybody talk about anything else?"

"Sure," said Olly. "I do religion and politics. Aquatic mammals, flowers, modern dance and..." She was staring as if he should be sectioned, so he needed a big finish. "Impressionism, post-modernism and baking." He grinned. "Brownies, anyway. The cakes, not the association for small girls. You were probably a patrol leader."

He couldn't read the pause but at least she didn't close the door. And the angle of her nose didn't lift. Behind her he noticed a suitcase and some carrier bags. Some expensive, shiny shoes pointed out of one of them, the kind his dad wore for work.

"I was a Scout," she said, "until a couple of months ago. Never saw you rock climbing or pot holing."

"My agility is mental."

"I've heard that word used about you. Not agility," she said, and her timing was perfect. "Mental."

"A legend in my own lifetime."

"I'm busy," said Eleanor. "Did you call round for anything in particular?"

"Too busy for a street party to end all street parties?" he asked, "probably forever."

"Are you drunk or do you always talk like this?"

"No, and yes, sometimes."

Eleanor sighed but Olly didn't really think she was bored. He reckoned he had to be more entertaining than revision. Or parental split-ups.

"Did James Allnutt put his spin on our date? So-called."

Olly hadn't seen that coming.

"No spin," he said. "So the date didn't work out? He bit off more than he could chew?"

She looked as if she'd never heard the phrase, which could be because people his age didn't use it.

"I like to do the biting."

She smiled, very briefly. Olly thought it took off two years, three, but added more than she could know. It was enough.

"That's serendipitous," he said, slowly, lifting the word at the end like an announcement at a prize giving. "Because I'm seriously chewy."

But not as mad as this. Not normally. It demanded an explanation.

"Look," she said, "give me five, OK?"

Which was just as well because he'd been about to tell her his granddad died today and that wouldn't be fair. She'd gone upstairs and he heard raised voices. Hers, sharp. Her father's, sharper. But the music blocked out the words. Then it stopped and the silence cut in, more like death than music could ever be. Olly had a feeling in his stomach that could be a misgiving, or a whole crowd of them.

"Enjoy the party," said Eleanor's mother from the landing, as if she had no hope of enjoying anything again.

Eleanor didn't say goodbye. In fact she didn't speak at all as she shut the door rather loudly. Olly's three penny bit felt cold above his chest.

Faith gave her mother a hug that was long and tight. She realised as it ended that the last one of its kind was after a cold and wet school trip to Windermere when she was twelve. The girl she shared with had wanted to be roomed with Shaz, and they'd both blamed her when the teachers wouldn't do a swap.

"Are you all right, sweetheart?"

For the first time that day, Faith felt the tears come. Mums had that effect and hers could probably name it like other syndromes. Then she wiped her cheeks and pulled herself free.

"No thanks to Tash and Ayesha."

Agnetha was embracing Stephen too, with much less excuse as far as Faith could see.

"I need contact numbers next time, Faith."

Faith wondered whether Agnetha knew she'd moved from stage one to stage two already in this particular behaviour pattern. From tender to firm.

"I might delete them both," she muttered, and supposed it was possible that the two of them had been trying to call her for hours and were feverish now with anxiety and guilt.

"You're fine. That's all that matters." Agnetha looked around, and Faith realised she'd remembered Hema. "But where...?"

"Ask James." Faith picked some rocket from her teeth. Then she started to sing, *"Love is in the air!"*

"Stephen? Have I missed something?"

"Only Dad dancing with Lucia," said Faith, and saw her father's shoulders sag with exasperation as he turned back from refilling his glass. "And me playing Cupid." She pretended to fire an arrow. "I think I may have hit the target twice. It's harder to tell with Hema but she was smiling rather a lot."

"Lovely girl," said Stephen, indistinctly. A celery stick between his teeth was tearing but refusing to snap.

"Where are they?" asked Agnetha.

"Gretna Green?" suggested Faith. "Vegas? Your bedroom?"

"I think," said Agnetha, and Faith recognised the tone at once, "you need to take a breath, darling."

"Sorry. Not your bedroom."

Her mother asked her father whether she'd been drinking.

"About five millilitres!" she protested.

Stephen said James had offered to take Hema home, but Faith didn't hear any more because Olly Jordan, the most annoying but interesting of all her brother's friends, was doing his wide-legged trundle towards them, with Eleanor Langridge overtopping him in heels and a dress made for shimmying.

"She'll eat him alive," escaped from Stephen.

"You're drunk, then," said Faith, and shook her head at him.

"Hello, Eleanor. What a gorgeous dress," Agnetha greeted her. She lowered her voice for Olly. "I won't ask how you're doing, Olly. I'm so sorry. You and Heinz had something... unusual."

"Thanks," said Olly. "Yeah. Yeah, we did."

Faith could see Eleanor didn't have a clue what she was talking about. Poor Olly. She gave him a smile that was meant to be sympathetic, about Heinz – and Eleanor too.

"If you find James hiding in a bush, Olly," said Agnetha, "would you send him over?"

"I keep telling you, Mum!" cried Faith. "They've gone." The music stopped while she was adding, "Probably to a street party. A proper one."

As he walked alongside Hema, James realised he had never been so aware of anyone's physical self and how little air there was to separate him from it. Her arm had already brushed his own, or his hers, more than once. Her spare hand was close enough to hold and it didn't take much imagination to feel the fingers curving round inside his.

James liked to walk by the South Bank, in Brick Lane and Camden: places where people were always in street party mood and it felt fine to be alone. In fact, better –

because it was the only way to observe with all senses, and take the experience neat, undiluted by chat. This was a different kind of walk because it wasn't the route he was drinking in, but her. What she saw, yes, and said – and what she might be thinking. Feeling.

It was further than his father had made out but between them they didn't need the A – Z except as back-up. And in a way the whole of it felt like a party, even in the places where life was ordinary and the late-night shops were open as always, with customers choosing plantains and cabbages from the pavement displays, waiting for chips or carrying out bags chinking with beer.

"There's more give in the air," he said. "I mean a kind of stretch. Elasticity. Not so tight."

Hema smiled. "Yes," she said, thinking how clever he was, whatever he said about exams and studying. "I feel it."

Was that what it was all about – a way of looking at the world, together but through the other person's eyes? Connecting. The media got it wrong, missed out on that. Not just touch and heat but *being,* shared.

Now he knew what it meant. But what would she say, James wondered, if he told her before they parted, *"I love you."*

"Whoah, boy!" Olly in his head. *"Crazy stuff! Steady."*

"You're sixteen, darling. Take it slowly. Life has many beginnings and endings." Agnetha. He sometimes thought she had these words of wisdom on cards like the ones people used for Shakespeare quotes and Acts of Parliament, dated. Filed with colour-coding. A message for every emotional scenario.

"The highest teenage pregnancy rate in Europe." His father – part of the talk, way too soon, very embarrassing, excess to requirements.

95

James looked at Hema as she pointed out the flowers in pots outside a restaurant and murmured that everything was out early because April had been so warm. She spoke quietly, but intently.

"I love gardens," she said. "Regent's Park. That's my favourite, when the roses are out."

If they came early too, it wouldn't be long. The two of them could go together. But he didn't dare say, assume.

Hema had never met a boy who would want to smell the roses too. She wished she could tell him she hoped they would spend the summer together. And the winter that followed.

"My father puts his head out when it's raining on the window boxes," she said. "He's had enough sun. He likes water on his skin."

She had told him a little about Mauritius, but felt a fraud because she was a tourist there too, without the five star hotel he'd stayed in. She had friends who dated boys from all kinds of backgrounds, and some of them spoke other languages, but she didn't know anyone with a boyfriend like James Allnutt. There was no one at her school with a home or voice like his.

"How did your parents meet?" she asked him, and then tried not to blush because of the implications. She hoped the tone was casual enough not to alarm him.

"At a wedding," he said, and smiled. "Somebody was match-making and put them at the same table."

"Somebody who knew them well, then, and thought they would be right."

"Yes," he said. "Quite a free gift, really. What about yours?"

"My mum was a nurse. My father worked as a hospital porter then. The way she tells it he had to chase her for months with a trolley."

Hema realised they weren't far from home and she should call, but that meant he would hear. She'd have to keep the facts minimal.

James realised as she produced her phone that it was the first time he'd seen it since she arrived at the party. Faith was addicted. She took hers to the loo, and it flickered like a candle all through every meal time. Hema's fingers were more deliberate.

"Hi, Mum!"

"Are you on the way home?"

"Yes. Ten minutes."

James could hear a warm, sympathetic voice telling her she must be tired.

"I'm fine. And I've had plenty to eat."

"You'll be hungry, both of you. There's plenty."

"See you soon, Mum."

She clicked off and smiled sheepishly. "She thinks I'm with Anant."

"Ah."

"I couldn't tell her all that on the phone. I just sent a text to say *Taking a young girl home. No problem but back late.*"

"Would she worry if she knew?"

"You heard her," she said, wondering what would happen at her street. Her door. "She's a worrier. Since she stopped work she hasn't had much else to do except worry. She even worries about the crises of all the characters in the soaps."

"That's a full time job!"

She laughed. They both liked their parents. It wasn't as common as she used to think.

For a while they'd been hearing a rhythm that grew stronger. Now the street they turned into was a loud one.

A steel band – one of Hema's favourite sounds because of the way people moved to the beat, as if they were on a beach. It was like walking into a market. The air was spiced, and thick with new warmth.

"Look!" said James, because in a full length white wedding gown and sunglasses was a tall, thin man, dancing in a way his dad would call jiggling.

Small children chased a cat across chalk pictures on the road, until it disappeared under the legs of a table covered in a Wills and Kate tablecloth. The nearest royal smile was creased and smeared with chutney. Lurching across the street was a bouncy castle, pink as strawberry mousse. At least one of the males flung from one wall to another was way over the age limit and roaring good-humouredly.

"Do you think it's for residents only?" Hema asked.

A woman in a green sari turned and handed them tissue flowers, a little tired and torn. "Welcome," she said. "Everyone is welcome. No strangers here."

"Great," said James. "Thanks." Holding the battered cerise flower to his nose, he pretended to breathe the scent. Then he poked the paper stem through a button hole.

Hema's hips had started to sway – just a little, and slowly.

"Shall we?" he asked, and held out his hand.

Hema nodded, and took it. For a moment she closed her eyes so that the drum beat could work its way through. She felt a smile twitch, lift and curve as he lifted her hand higher and pulled her under. Her hair stroked his cheek, his chest.

They were dancing.

Lightning Source UK Ltd.
Milton Keynes UK
UKOW040927280912

199730UK00002B/2/P